GRISLY

To save their clan, young warrior Bran O'Neal and the elf Neal O'Neal must find Bran's missing brother, and the lost Sword of the O'Neal's, the Reaper. But their hunt leads to a forest teeming with dragons, gremlins, ogres, giants, monkey-frogs, rat-things, spider men, and dog men—all impossible minions of an unknown, malevolent wizard. This wizard's been making monsters . . . many monsters, and he has some special plans for Bran—special torments, special combats, and an inconceivable destiny from beyond space . . .

CROSSROADS™ ADVENTURES are authorized interactive novels compatible for use with any role-playing game. Constructed by the masters of modern gaming, CROSSROADS™ feature complete rules; *full use* of gaming values—strength, intelligence, wisdom/luck, constitution, dexterity, charisma and hit points; and multiple pathways for each option; for the most complete experience in gaming books, as fully realised, motivated heroes quest through the most famous worlds of fantasy!

With an all-new introduction by Christopher Stasheff

ENTER THE ADVENTURE

TOR'S CROSSROADS ADVENTURE SERIES

A CROSSROADS ADVENTURE

in the World of
CHRISTOPHER STASHEFF'S
WARLOCK OF GRAMARYE

A WARLOCK'S BLADE

by Mark Perry
with Megahn Perry

A TOM DOHERTY ASSOCIATES BOOK

A WARLOCK'S BLADE

Copyright © 1987 Bill Fawcett and Associates

Crossroads Game/novels are published by TOR Books by arrangement with Bill Fawcett and Associates.

First printing: December 1987

A TOR Book

Published by Tom Doherty Associates, Inc.
49 West 24th Street
New York, NY 10010

Cover art by Doug Beekman

Illustrations by Todd Cameron Hamilton

ISBN: 0-812-56413-8
CAN. No.: 0-812-56414-6

Printed in the United States of America

0 9 8 7 6 5 4 3 2 1

This book is dedicated to Michael T. Perry

INTRODUCTION TO GRAMARYE

and the *Warlock* Series

of Novels

by

Christopher Stasheff

BY 3150 A.D., the people of Terra had expanded to infest a dozen or twenty planets. The mother world had managed to keep all her children in one big, more-or-less happy family by banding them together into a democracy called the Interstellar Dominion Electorates. But democracy requires speedy exchange of information, and the Terran Sphere was becoming too large for the speed of its communications. The I.D.E. went into a decline, and a few idealists saw the end of freedom coming. They managed to buy a used spaceship and stock it with a quorum of members of the Society for Creative Anachronism, and take off for parts unknown just before a reactionary coup destroyed the I.D.E.

They changed their name to the Romantic Emigres and decided to get lost—and when SCA people decide to do something, they generally do a pretty thorough job of it. They were so thorough that, for five hundred years, Terra lost track of them. Meanwhile, they picked out a nice G-type sun with a planet about one astronomical unit away and engineered the climate and the plant life of one large island to resemble Terra's. Then they proceeded to lose track of Terra by having a computer erase all memories of post-Medieval technology from their minds and implant new names and backgrounds—those of their SCA personas. The result was an agglomerate medieval culture, with a wonderful hodge-podge of styles and nationalities, all blended into one glorious utopia.

Then the worm began to gnaw. Barons began to lord it over their serfs, as barons are wont to do, and began to pay the King a fine medieval disregard. And when the second generation hit puberty, some very strange things began to happen. The occasional teenage girl took off for a night flight on a broomstick, and the odd teenage boy couldn't keep his feet on the ground. Sometimes he was *very* odd—even became rather flighty. When his parents tried to bring him down to earth, he tended to disappear in a cloud of dust, or at least a thunderclap. But most of his peers didn't think the performance rated such applause—they raised the hue and cry and declared open season on witches. They did manage to find a few, who got really burned up about it, but most of the magical adolescents disappeared into the tall timber (well, not *very* tall yet, but it was pretty dense). Finally, the mob realized that the alarm had passed from witch to witch with the speed of thought—in fact, *as* thought; the witchlings were telepaths!

Their contemporaries weren't about to take this calmly, of course—after all, if it was different, it might be superior, and no one wants to take a chance on being outclassed. So witch-hunting became a great national pastime, second only to jousting and other forms of mayhem. The hunters even occasionally caught something.

Sometimes it caught them—because there was one native life-form that hadn't succumbed to the imported Terran plants and livestock. It was a telepathically sensitive fungus which the peasants called "witch-moss," because if the right kind of witch thought at it hard, it turned into whatever she was thinking about. It was such a good reproduction that it could even reproduce. It could also walk, swim, or fly, depending on its species, and could even talk, work magic, and think, if that's what its particular sort of monster was supposed to be able to do. And there were a great many monsters, of course—anything that a person with an active imagination could dream up, or remember from a story they'd once heard. So all the magical creatures of Terran folklore tended to show up somewhere on the island, sooner or later—elves, werewolves, banshees, faerie folk, and suchlike—plus some highly original creations, on top of it all.

So their descendants had a high old time, hunting and feasting and fighting—except for the peasants, when the crops failed; and everybody, when a plague hit; and anybody who happened to be born into an estate run by an evil lord. Because, when the Romantic Emigres forgot about technology, they also forgot about such frills as legal codes, modern medicine, and freedom. This was all ameliorated somewhat by a corps of monks, priests, and brothers of the Order of St. Vidicon of Cathode, who managed to spread the balm of Christianity and its restraining notion of chivalry; but there was just so much they could do.

And that's how matters stood after five hundred years, when the Terran planets, unbeknown to the good folk of Gramarye, managed to throw off the chains of dictatorship and reestablish an enlightened government called the Decentralized Democratic Tribunal. It was a lively, vital form of political life, rooted in total literacy, saturated by an astonishingly high level of education, and breathing the heady ambience of faster-than-light radio. But it was expanding at an alarming rate as it discovered Lost Colonies and absorbed them back into the mainstream of life. It needed virtually instant communications—if it was going to survive—and it found them, in Gramarye's telepaths.

Unfortunately, so did two other organizations —the Vigilant Exterminators of Telepathic Organisms (VETO), dedicated to converting the Terran planets to dictatorships; and the Society for the Prevention of Telepathic Entities (SPITE), devoted to the destruction of all governments and the triumph of anarchy. The two organizations couldn't agree on much, but they made an exception in the case of democracy. They both knew that no matter what might bring triumph, democracy would bring disaster, and that Gramarye's telepaths might make democracy permanent. So they focused all their attention on destroying anything on Gramarye that might resemble a budding constitution, such as a king gaining enough power to keep the barons from tearing the land apart with continual pocket wars. Whenever they found a promising candidate, they managed to kill him off. They were so successful, in fact, that the Royal Family was finally down to one daughter—Queen Catharine, a strong-willed young lady who had plans for her country. So VETO and SPITE had plans for her.

But none of their plans included Rod Gallowglass.

Rod Gallowglass was the man who found Gramarye for Terra. That was his job—he was a secret agent for the DDT's Society for the Conversion of Extraterrestrial Nascent Totalitarianisms, specializing in finding Lost Colonies that might turn into dictatorships and subverting them back into democracies. He more than had his work cut out for him, but he realized how important Gramarye was to the future of democracy, so he was ready to devote his whole life to it. He also wound up devoting his life to a high-powered witch named Gwendylon and their four children, but that's another story. Many of them, in fact.

The story in this book, though, was going on while Rod was meeting Catharine and Gwendylon. It was one of those skirmishes that go on far away from the main battles in a war, so they aren't remembered much, even though they set up the good guys for the big victories. The people who win them are just as much heroes as the famous ones, even though their sagas aren't generally sung. They have to make do with self-esteem and, sometimes, living happily ever after.

Sometimes . . .

INTRODUCTION
AND RULES
TO CROSSROADS™
ADVENTURES
by Bill Fawcett

FOR THE MANY of us who have enjoyed the stories upon which this adventure is based, it may seem a bit strange to find an introduction this long at the start of a book. What you are holding is both a game and an adventure. Have you ever read a book and then told yourself you would have been able to think more clearly or seen a way out of the hero's dilemma? In a Crossroads™ adventure you have the opportunity to do just that. *You* make the key decisions. By means of a few easily followed steps you are able to see the results of your choices.

A Crossroads™ adventure is as much fun to read as it is to play. It is more than just a game or a book. It is a chance to enjoy once more a familiar and treasured story. The excitement of adventuring in a beloved universe is neatly blended into a story which stands well on its own merit, a story in which you will encounter many familiar characters and places and discover more than a few new ones as well. Each adventure is a thrilling tale, with the extra suspense and satisfaction of knowing that you will succeed or fail by your own endeavors.

THE ADVENTURE

Throughout the story you will have the opportunity to make decisions. Each of these decisions will affect whether the hero succeeds in the quest, or even survives. In some cases you will actually be fighting battles; other times you will use your knowledge and instincts to choose the best path to follow. In many cases there will be clues in the story or illustrations.

A Crossroads™ adventure is divided into sections. The length of a section may be a few lines or many pages. The section numbers are shown at the top of a page to make it easier for you to follow. Each section ends when you must make a decision, or fight. The next section you turn to will show the results of your decision. At least one six-sided die and a pencil are needed to "play" this book.

The words "six-sided dice" are often abbreviated as "D6." If more than one is needed a number will precede the term. "Roll three six-sided dice" will be written as "Roll 3 D6." Virtually all the die rolls in these rules do involve rolling three six-sided dice (or rolling one six-sided die three times) and totaling what is rolled.

If you are an experienced role-play gamer, you may also wish to convert the values given in this novel to those you can use with any fantasy role-playing game you are now playing with. All of the adventures have been constructed so that they also can be easily adapted in this manner. The values for the hero may transfer directly. While fantasy games are much more complicated, doing this will allow you to be the Game Master for other players. Important values for the hero's opponents will be given to aid you in this conversion and to give those playing by the Crossroads™ rules a better idea of what they are facing.

THE HERO

Seven values are used to describe the hero in gaming terms. These are strength, intelligence, wisdom/luck, constitution, dexterity, charisma, and hit points. These values measure all of a character's abilities. At the end of these rules is a record sheet. On it are given all of the values for the hero of this adventure and any equipment or supplies they begin the adventure with. While you adventure, this record can be used to keep track of damage received and any new equipment or magical items acquired. You may find it advisable to make a photocopy of that page. Permission to do so, for your own use only, is given by the publisher of this game/novel. You may wish to consult this record sheet as we discuss what each of the values represents.

STRENGTH

This is the measure of how physically powerful your hero is. It compares the hero to others in how much the character can lift, how hard he can punch, and just how brawny he is. The strongest a normal human can be is to have a strength value of 18. The weakest a child would have is a 3. Here is a table giving comparable strengths:

Strength	Example
3	A 5-year-old child
6	An elderly man
8	Out of shape and over 40
10	An average 20-year-old man
13	In good shape and works out
15	A top athlete or football running back
17	Changes auto tires without a jack
18	Arm wrestles Arnold Schwarzenegger and wins

A Tolkien-style troll, being magical, might have a strength of 19 or 20. A full-grown elephant has a strength of 23. A fifty-foot dragon would have a strength of 30.

INTELLIGENCE

Being intelligent is not just a measure of native brain power. It is also an indication of the ability to use that intelligence. The value for intelligence also measures how aware the character is, and so how likely they are to notice a subtle clue. Intelligence can be used to measure how resistant a mind is to hypnosis or mental attack. A really sharp baboon would have an intelligence of 3. Most humans (we all know exceptions) begin at about 5. The highest value possible is an 18. Here is a table of relative intelligence:

Intelligence	Example
3	My dog
5	Lassie
6	Curly (the third Stooge)
8	Somewhat slow
10	Average person
13	College professor/good quarterback
15	Indiana Jones/Carl Sagan
17	Doc Savage/Mr. Spock
18	Leonardo dá Vinci (Isaac Asimov?)

Brainiac of comic-book fame would have a value of 21.

WISDOM/LUCK

Wisdom is the ability to make correct judgments, often with less than complete facts. Wisdom is knowing what to do and when to do it. Attacking, when running will earn you a spear in the back, is the best part of wisdom. Being in the right place at the right time can be called luck or wisdom. Not being discovered when hiding can be luck, if it is because you knew enough to not hide in the poison oak, wisdom is also a factor. Activities which are based more on instinct, the intuitive leap, than analysis are decided by wisdom.

In many ways both wisdom and luck are further connected, especially as wisdom also measures how friendly the ruling powers of the universe (not the author, the fates) are to the hero. A hero may be favored by fate or luck because he is reverent or for no discernible reason at all. This will give him a high wisdom value. Everyone knows those "lucky" individuals who can fall in the mud and find a gold coin. Here is a table measuring relative wisdom/luck:

Wisdom	Example
Under 3	Cursed or totally unthinking

5	Never plans, just reacts
7	Some cunning, "street smarts"
9	Average thinking person
11	Skillful planner, good gambler
13	Successful businessman/Lee Iacocca
15	Captain Kirk (wisdom)/Conan (luck)
17	Sherlock Holmes (wisdom)/Luke Skywalker (luck)
18	Lazarus Long

CONSTITUTION

The more you can endure, the higher your constitution. If you have a high constitution you are better able to survive physical damage, emotional stress, and poisons. The higher your value for constitution, the longer you are able to continue functioning in a difficult situation. A character with a high constitution can run farther (though not necessarily faster) or hang by one hand longer than the average person. A high constitution means you also have more stamina, and recover more quickly from injuries. A comparison of values for constitution:

Constitution	Example
3	A terminal invalid
6	A 10-year-old child

8	Your stereotyped "98-pound weakling"
10	Average person
14	Olympic athlete/Sam Spade
16	Marathon runner/Rocky
18	Rasputin/Batman

A whale would have a constitution of 20. Superman's must be about 50.

DEXTERITY

The value for dexterity measures not only how fast a character can move, but how well-coordinated those movements are. A surgeon, a pianist, and a juggler all need a high value for dexterity. If you have a high value for dexterity you can react quickly (though not necessarily correctly), duck well, and perform sleight-of-hand magic (if you are bright enough to learn how). Conversely, a low dexterity means you react slowly and drop things frequently. All other things being equal, the character with the highest dexterity will have the advantage of the first attack in a combat. Here are some comparative examples of dexterity:

Dexterity	Example
3 or less	Complete klutz
5	Inspector Clousseau

6	Can walk and chew gum, most of the time
8	Barney Fife
10	Average person
13	Good fencer/Walter Payton
15	Brain surgeon/Houdini
16	Flying Karamazov Brothers
17	Movie ninja/Cyrano de Bergerac
18	Bruce Lee

Batman, Robin, Daredevil and The Shadow all have a dexterity of 19. At a dexterity of 20 you don't even see the man move before he has taken your wallet and underwear and has left the room (the Waco Kid).

CHARISMA

Charisma is more than just good looks, though they certainly don't hurt. It is a measure of how persuasive a hero is and how willing others are to do what he wants. You can have average looks yet be very persuasive, and have a high charisma. If your value for charisma is high, you are better able to talk yourself out of trouble or obtain information from a stranger. If your charisma is low, you may be ignored or even mocked, even when you are right. A high charisma value is vital to entertainers of any sort, and leaders. A different type of charisma is just as important to spies.

In the final measure a high value for charisma means people will react to you in the way you desire. Here are some comparative values for charisma:

Charisma	Example
3	Hunchback of Notre Dame
5	An ugly used-car salesman
7	Richard Nixon today
10	Average person
12	Team coach
14	Magnum, P.I.
16	Henry Kissinger/Jim DiGriz
18	Dr. Who/Prof. Harold Hill (Centauri)

HIT POINTS

Hit points represent the total amount of damage a hero can take before he is killed or knocked out. You can receive damage from being wounded in a battle, through starvation, or even through a mental attack. Hit points measure more than just how many times the hero can be battered over the head before he is knocked out. They also represent the ability to keep striving toward a goal. A poorly paid mercenary may have only a few hit points, even though he is a hulking brute of a man, because the first time he receives even a slight wound he will withdraw from the fight. A blacksmith's apprentice who won't accept defeat will have a higher number of hit points.

A character's hit points can be lost through a wound to a specific part of the body or through general damage to the body itself. This general damage can be caused by a poison, a bad fall, or even exhaustion and starvation. Pushing your body too far beyond its limits may result in a successful action at the price of the loss of a few hit points. All these losses are treated in the same manner.

Hit points lost are subtracted from the total on the hero's record sheet. When a hero has lost all of his hit points, then that character has failed. When this happens you will be told to which section to turn. Here you will often find a description of the failure and its consequences for the hero.

The hit points for the opponents the hero meets in combat are given in the adventure. You should keep track of these hit points on a piece of scrap paper. When a monster or opponent has lost all of their hit points, they have lost the fight. If a character is fighting more than one opponent, then you should keep track of each of their hit points. Each will continue to fight until it has 0 hit points. When everyone on one side of the battle has no hit points left, the combat is over.

Even the best played character can lose all of his hit points when you roll too many bad dice during a combat. If the hero loses all of his hit points, the adventure may have ended in failure.

You will be told so in the next section you are instructed to turn to. In this case you can turn back to the first section and begin again. This time you will have the advantage of having learned some of the hazards the hero will face.

TAKING CHANCES

There will be occasions where you will have to decide whether the hero should attempt to perform some action which involves risk. This might be to climb a steep cliff, jump a pit, or juggle three daggers. There will be other cases where it might benefit the hero to notice something subtle or remember an ancient ballad perfectly. In all of these cases you will be asked to roll three six-sided dice (3 D6) and compare the total of all three dice to the hero's value for the appropriate ability.

For example, if the hero is attempting to juggle three balls, then for him to do so successfully you would have to roll a total equal to or less than the hero's value for dexterity. If your total was less than this dexterity value, then you would be directed to a section describing how the balls looked as they were skillfully juggled. If you rolled a higher value than that for dexterity, then you would be told to read a section which describes the embarrassment of dropping the balls, and being laughed at by the audience.

Where the decision is a judgment call, such as whether to take the left or right staircase, it is left entirely to you. Somewhere in the adventure or in the original novels there will be some piece of information which would indicate that the left staircase leads to a trap and the right to your goal. No die roll will be needed for a judgment decision.

In all cases you will be guided at the end of each section as to exactly what you need do. If you have any questions you should refer back to these rules.

MAGICAL ITEMS AND SPECIAL EQUIPMENT

There are many unusual items which appear in the pages of this adventure. When it is possible for them to be taken by the hero, you will be given the option of doing so. One or more of these items may be necessary to the successful completion of the adventure. You will be given the option of taking these at the end of a section. If you choose to pick up an item and succeed in getting it, you should list that item on the hero's record sheet. There is no guarantee that deciding to take an item means you will actually obtain it. If someone owns it already they are quite likely to resent your efforts to take it. In some cases things may not even be all they appear to be or the item may be trapped or cursed. Having it may prove a detriment rather than a benefit.

All magical items give the hero a bonus (or penalty) on certain die rolls. You will be told when this applies, and often given the option of whether or not to use the item. You will be instructed at the end of the section on how many points to add to or subtract from your die roll. If you choose to use an item which can function only once, such as a magic potion or hand grenade, then you will also be instructed to remove the item from your record sheet. Certain items, such as a magic sword, can be used many times. In this case you will be told when you obtain the item when you can apply the bonus. The bonus for a magic sword could be added every time a character is in hand-to-hand combat.

Other special items may allow a character to fly, walk through fire, summon magical warriors, or many other things. How and when they affect play will again be told to you in the paragraphs at the end of the sections where you have the choice of using them.

Those things which restore lost hit points are a special case. You may choose to use these at any time during the adventure. If you have a magical healing potion which returns 1 D6 of lost hit points, you may add these points when you think it is best to. This can even be during a combat in the place of a round of attack. No matter how many healing items you use, a character can never have more hit points than he begins the adventure with.

There is a limit to the number of special items any character may carry. In any Crossroads™ adventure the limit is four items. If you already have four special items listed on your record sheet, then one of these must be discarded in order to take the new item. Any time you erase an item off the record sheet, whether because it was used or because you wish to add a new item, whatever is erased is permanently lost. It can never be "found" again, even if you return to the same location later in the adventure.

Except for items which restore hit points, the hero can only use an item in combat or when given the option to do so. The opportunity will be listed in the instructions.

In the case of an item which can be used in every combat, the bonus can be added or subtracted as the description of the item indicates. A +2 sword would add two points to any total rolled in combat. This bonus would be used each and every time the hero attacks. Only one attack bonus can be used at a time. Just because a hero has both a +1 and a +2 sword doesn't mean he knows how to fight with both at once. Only the better bonus would apply.

If a total of 12 is needed to hit an attacking monster and the hero has a +2 sword, then you will only need to roll a total of 10 on the three dice to successfully strike the creature.

You could also find an item, perhaps enchanted armor, which could be worn in all combat and would have the effect of subtracting its bonus from the total of any opponent's attack on its wearer. (Bad guys can wear magic armor, too.) If a monster normally would need a 13 to hit a character who has obtained a set of +2 armor, then the monster would now need a total of 15 to score a hit. An enchanted shield would operate in the same way, but could never be used when the character was using a weapon which needed both hands, such as a pike, longbow, or two-handed sword.

COMBAT

There will be many situations where the hero will be forced, or you may choose, to meet an opponent in combat. The opponents can vary from a wild beast, to a human thief, or an unearthly monster. In all cases the same steps are followed.

The hero will attack first in most combats unless you are told otherwise. This may happen when there is an ambush, other special situations, or because the opponent simply has a much higher dexterity.

At the beginning of a combat section you will be given the name or type of opponent involved. For each combat five values are given. The first of these is the total on three six-sided dice needed for the attacker to hit the hero. Next to this value is the value the hero needs to hit these opponents. After these two values is listed the hit points of the opponent. If there is more than one opponent, each one will have the same number. (See the Hit Points section included earlier if you are unclear as to what these do.) Under the value needed to be hit by the opponent is the hit points of damage that it will do to the hero when it attacks successfully. Finally, under the total needed for the hero to successfully hit an opponent is the damage he will do with the different weapons he might have. Unlike a check for completing a daring action (where you wish to roll under a value), in a combat you have to roll the value given or higher on three six-sided dice to successfully hit an opponent.

For example:

Here is how a combat between the hero armed with a sword and three brigands armed only with daggers is written:

BRIGANDS

To hit the hero: 14   To be hit: 12   Hit points: 4
Damage with   Damage with
daggers: 1 D6   sword: 2 D6
(used by the brigands) (used by the hero)
There are three brigands. If two are killed (taken to 0 hit points) the third will flee in panic.

If the hero wins, turn to section 85.

If he is defeated, turn to section 67.

RUNNING AWAY

Running rather than fighting, while often desirable, is not always possible. The option to run away is available only when listed in the choices. Even when this option is given, there is no guarantee the hero can get away safely.

THE COMBAT SEQUENCE

Any combat is divided into alternating rounds. In most cases the hero will attack first. Next, surviving opponents will have the chance to fight back. When both have attacked, one round will have been completed. A combat can have any number of rounds and continues until the hero or his opponents are defeated. Each round is the equivalent of six seconds. During this time all the parties in the combat may actually take more than one swing at each other.

The steps in resolving a combat in which the hero attacks first are as follows:

1. Roll three six-sided dice. Total the numbers showing on all three and add any bonuses from weapons or special circumstances. If

this total is the same or greater than the second value given, "to hit the opponent," then the hero has successfully attacked.

2. If the hero attacks successfully, the next step is to determine how many hit points of damage he did to the opponent. The die roll for this will be given below the "to hit opponent" information.

3. Subtract any hit points of damage done from the opponent's total.

4. If any of the enemy have one or more hit points left, then the remaining opponent or opponents now can attack. Roll three six-sided dice for each attacker. Add up each of these sets of three dice. If the total is the same as, or greater than the value listed after "to hit the hero" in the section describing the combat, the attack was successful.

5. For each hit, roll the number of dice listed for damage. Subtract the total from the number of hit points the hero has at that time. Enter the new, lower total on the hero's record sheet.

If both the hero and one or more opponents have hit points left, the combat continues. Start again at step one. The battle ends only when the hero is killed, all the opponents are killed, or all

of one side has run away. A hero cannot, except
through a healing potion or spells or when specifically told to during the adventure, regain lost hit
points. A number of small wounds from several
opponents will kill a character as thoroughly as
one titanic, unsuccessful combat with a hill
giant.

DAMAGE

The combat continues, following the sequence
given below, until either the hero or his opponents have no hit points. In the case of multiple
opponents, subtract hit points from one opponent until the total reaches 0 or less. Extra hit
points of damage done on the round when each
opponent is defeated are lost. They do not carry
over to the next enemy in the group. To win the
combat, you must eliminate all of an opponent's
hit points.

The damage done by a weapon will vary depending on who is using it. A club in the hands of
a child will do far less damage than the same club
wielded by a hill giant. The maximum damage is
given as a number of six-sided dice. In some
cases the maximum will be less than a whole die.
This is abbreviated by a minus sign followed by a
number. For example D6−2, meaning one roll of
a six-sided die, minus two. The total damage can
never be less than zero, meaning no damage
done. 2 D6−1 means that you should roll two

six-sided dice and then subtract one from the total of them both.

A combat may, because of the opponent involved, have one or more special circumstances. It may be that the enemy will surrender or flee when its hit point total falls below a certain level, or even that reinforcements will arrive to help the bad guys after so many rounds. You will be told of these special situations in the lines directly under the combat values.

Now you may turn to section 1.

RECORD SHEET
Bran O'Neal—Knight Errant

Strength: 15
Intelligence: 13
Wisdom/Luck: 17
Constitution: 14
Dexterity: 17
Charisma: 10

Hit Points: 30
Magical Items:
1. chainmail +2
2.
3.
4.

Weapons Carried:
long sword
short sword
dagger

Bran has limited magic ability. He has mastered two spells:
1. A HEALING spell that he can use twice a day. He may use it before, after, or during battle. It cures him of 1–3 hit points of damage.
2. A MISDIRECTION spell that he can do three times a day. It can be used only during combat (taking a battle round to complete.) The spell subtracts 2 from an enemy's chance to hit him. It lasts one battle round.

* **1** *

Bran O'Neal warily follows his father Rory into the great hall of their liege lord, Duke Loguire. The room is immense, lit by torches inset in silver sconces along its length. A silver chandelier hangs from the concave roof, spreading light on the Loguire coat of arms inlaid on the stone floor.

Bran whistles softly to himself at his first sight of all the Great Lords of the Kingdom assembled with their vassals in the great hall. It hasn't escaped the young warrior that all within are heavily armed. His father's warning from the night before echoes within him: "There is base treachery behind this council." Bran grasps his sword hilt tightly.

As Sir Rory O'Neal moves through the mass of people the other lords make way for him, grudgingly, but many eyes watch the old baronet's back as if wishing a sharp dagger lodged there. Rory is aware but moves on unflinchingly toward the dais at the end of the hall where Duke Loguire sits, his great frame tense as he gauges the mood of his peers. Suddenly a figure stands, unmoving, in front of them. It is one of the mysterious, gnomish men who have appeared from some unknown land. As far as Bran knows, only his father has refused their services, distrusting their counsel from the first.

"Out of my way, villain." Rory's voice is harsh.

"Ah, my lord, I mean no disrespect—" But the councillor's tone and manner belies his words. "I simply offer my help."

"I need no help from such as you." He moves his hand to the hilt of his sword for emphasis.

"It seems you do, my lord." The councillor rubs his hands together, his eyes fixed on Rory's hand where it grips his sword hilt. "There is decorum in all things, my lord, and in council all have their place. Yours, I fear, is not so near the front." A few snicker at that. The councillor gives a bow, too deep to be intended as anything but an insult. "Let me show you your rightful place, my good lord." As the man reaches out to grasp Rory's shoulder, something in the baronet's dark eyes restrains him. Instead, the councillor gestures grandly, and without looking back marches toward the rear of the hall.

The old warrior has no choice but to follow, though he grits his teeth in anger. Bran, too, dislikes this turn of events. His father tried to break tradition, true, but for good reason; fear for his liege lord, the Loguire. Any who wish the duke ill would naturally want the O'Neal, and his son, as far from the duke as possible since the O'Neals are reputed to be the finest warriors on Gramarye.

The councillor leads the two warriors to a back corner and leaves them there. Bran bites his lip; the situation looks grim. They are surrounded by knights whose colors are unfamiliar to him, though their liege lord is seemingly the Duke of Bourbon, a man his father has no love for. Backed against a wall, surrounded on all sides by potential enemies, if something did go amiss, the O'Neals are in a poor position to help their liege.

To quiet his misgivings Bran reviews the situation as it was explained to him. This council was called without the Queen's knowledge. Here the lords of the land are to decide how to handle what they see as Queen Catharine's attempt to usurp their power.

They have cause for concern, Bran admits to himself. For the Queen recently decided that the land must have a more central system of justice and sent to each of the lords her own royal judges who were to rule on all disputes in any of the demesnes. Then she ruled that she and she alone had the right to choose who would enter the priesthood and where they would preach. Both of these rights had belonged to the individual peers of the realm since time unrecorded. No ruler had ever dared to try to constrain the individual power of the lords before.

Still, there is something amiss in the nobles' reaction to all this, Bran thinks to himself. True, the Queen is high-handed and her ideas are a bit unorthodox, but they do have merit and the Queen is within her rights. Some lords may use

Section 1

their hold on the law and religion to further their own power, at the expense of their peasants, but since the first O'Neal built the castle that Bran's father still rules, the family has been known for their evenhandedness in dealing with the underclass. Indeed, this stand has caused the O'Neals to clash with other nobles before now. It has also given the O'Neals power beyond their title's worth, for many of the peasants who escape the harsh rule of others choose to relocate on O'Neal land. And the O'Neal has a reason beyond loyalty to support the Queen, despite her excesses. Catharine is the first ruler of Gramarye to offer protection to witches and, though it is a close-kept secret, Bran's own mother, Elisabeth, is a witch. The O'Neal would dare almost anything to protect her.

Bran is shaken from his reverie by the Loguire's deep voice booming over the noise of the assembled lords.

He turns to his father for guidance. Rory's hands are tightly gripping the two swords of the O'Neal clan. His face is white. He turns to his son.

"They"—his voice breaks—"they wish to pull Catharine down." Even as he speaks the words, Lord Bourbon's voice growls.

"Nay, good cuz! We must pull her down."

"Aye," murmurs di Medici, and the other lords raise their voices in agreement.

A cry of "Aye" rolls through the hall as the assembled vassals take up the call.

The O'Neals' denial is lost amid that great clamor.

"Now I say, *Nay!*" Loguire roars.

Bran is stunned by it all. How could these great lords betray their rightful Queen. Can this be? Would they truly start a civil war? Again his thoughts are interrupted as the talk takes another turn.

"What king should we have but Anselm, Loguire's son?" says di Medici. Anselm? They are insane, Bran thinks. Anselm would make no strong king.

"Father—" He turns to his sire full of questions, but the old knight merely scowls at Bran for a moment to silence him. They are surrounded by enemies. The unfamiliar knights have all their attention on the argument at the other end of the hall, but one figure stands apart from the rest: one of the councillors. Whether it is the one who insulted his father, Bran cannot tell; in truth they all look the same to him. But he cannot miss the threat in the old one's birdlike eyes.

Another voice rises above the crowd. Bran knows that voice. It is the councillor to Duke Loguire himself.

"What say you, lord? Shall this man die?" There is a pause. Then, to Bran's horror, once again the hall rings with "Aye."

"I say thee nay!" Sir Rory O'Neal cries, drawing his two wicked blades. Bran quickly follows.

The councillor cries, "Kill them!" And the

knights about the O'Neals turn and draw their weapons.

"The verdict, my lords, is death," Durer says. Even as he finishes the sentence, Bran and his father wade into the group of traitor knights, their double swords whistling in tandem. Bran slices one man's throat, even as his father takes another in the heart.

And the lights go out.

"Quickly, Bran, out of here. We can't help the Loguire now." Bran follows the sound of his father's voice; his family's unique training allowing him to avoid the confused and milling knights. As he nears the entranceway he hears a voice behind him.

"Not so quickly, young serpent." It is one of the councillors. Bran turns to meet the threat. Somehow the councillor can sense his presence, even in the darkness of the hall, or worse, he may have some arcane sight which allows him to see in the dark. Bran grasps his swords tightly. He dares not run if the councillor can detect him. That will only earn him a knife in the back. His family's training comes to his aid again and though he cannot see his enemy, he *can* detect his presence. He feels no fear as he waits for the attack that must come.

COUNCILLOR
To hit Bran: 15   To be hit: 10   Hit Points: 6
Damage with knife: 1 D6+3 (3 more pts. of damage are added each time the councillor hits

due to the fact that the knife gives off an electrical charge).

Damage with swords (Bran's): 1 D6+2

If Bran defeats the councillor, turn to section 2.

If Bran is defeated by the councillor, turn to section 3.

* **2** *

Bran hears a rasping sound and then he is momentarily blinded by a sudden light. Instinctively he steps back and he feels the air rush past his face. The light becomes less intense and Bran realizes that the councillor's knife is glowing. What magic is this?

The wizened councillor waves the knife threateningly, the strange glow from the weapon reflecting off his face. The light highlights the almost inhuman features of the man. His skin is stretched tight, showing the skull beneath. Bran realizes that the councillor is old, old beyond imagining, and those dark eyes hide a knowledge far more frightening than the glowing knife.

Bran attacks with his long sword while he moves the short one to parry the councillor's magic knife. But the old one is nimble and evades Bran's attack. When the short sword connects with the knife, Bran feels a strange biting along his palm and momentarily his weapon glows in tandem with his enemy's. Three times Bran attacks, and three times the councillor deftly avoids Bran's flashing blades.

Bran is desperate. He can hear the clank of armor coming from the main hall and knows that the councillor seeks to hold him here until help arrives, but Bran dares not turn to escape. A knife in the back is no way for a true son of the O'Neals to die. He must make an end to his enemy before he can flee.

He attacks once more, but this time he only feints with the longsword, then parries the knife with the same weapon. The councillor is caught off guard, and Bran lunges at his enemy with the short sword. This time the councillor cannot get away and the weapon pierces his heart. Even as the blade steals the life from the old one, the warriors begin to relight the torches about the hall. Bran hears movement behind him and turns to meet this new threat.

"Hold on, lad," Rory says. He, too, holds the double swords of the O'Neals and red blood stains both blades. He nods to Bran. "Good work," he says, kicking the body of the councillor, "but there's more where that demon came from. Follow me. We must be away ere the traitors can rally." With that he turns and runs from the hall.

Bran follows and the two run together through the long halls of Loguire's mountain hold. They ignore the questions flung at them by the confused people they pass, and those who try to stop them are cut down by the flashing blades of father and son.

They pass through the front gates to where a handful of their retainers wait with saddled horses. They mount quickly.

As they urge their mounts into a gallop Bran shouts, "Father, what will this mean?"

His father cries above the pounding hoof beats.

"It means base treachery, my son. Aye, that and more. Treachery and red-handed war."

Record any damage Bran has taken and turn to section 4.

* **3** *

Bran hears a rasping sound and then is momentarily blinded by a sudden light. Instinctively, he steps back and he feels the air stir near his face. The light becomes less intense and Bran realizes that the councillor's knife is glowing. What magic is this?

The wizened councillor waves the knife threateningly, the strange glow from the weapon reflecting off his face. The light highlights the strong features of the man. His skin is stretched tight, showing the skull beneath. Bran realizes

Section 3

the councillor is old, old beyond imagining, and those dark eyes hide a knowledge far more frightening than the glowing knife.

Bran attacks with his long sword while he moves the short one to parry the councillor's magic knife. But the old one is nimble and evades Bran's attack. When the short sword connects with the knife, Bran feels a strange biting along his palm and momentarily his weapon glows in tandem with his enemy's. Three times Bran attacks, and three times the councillor deftly avoids Bran's flashing blades.

Bran is desperate. He can hear the clank of armor coming from the main hall and knows that the councillor seeks to hold him here until help arrives, but Bran dares not turn to escape. A knife in the back is not a way for a true son of the O'Neals to die. He must make an end to his enemy before he can flee.

Bran attacks once more, but this time he only feints with the long sword, then parries the knife with the same weapon. But the councillor recognizes the move. He realizes Bran means to attack with the short sword and defend with the long. The councillor drops his arm and Bran's parry sweeps harmlessly into the air. Before Bran can react, the councillor steps into the young warrior's guard and thrusts his knife deep into Bran's chest.

The pain is incredible. It is as if Bran's whole chest has been lit afire. Bran crashes to the ground, unable to control his cries as the magic from the deadly blade tears into his flesh, burning him with its power. The councillor leans over him. All Bran can see is dark eyes burning with victory, gloating over the young warrior's agony. Then all is dark.

Bran wakes to find his father standing over him. Rory's face is haggard and pale.

"I have used the spell your mother taught me, lad." His father's voice is hoarse. "It has taken much out of me to heal you, but you should be strong enough to follow me. Hurry, we must flee this place or die."

Bran lifts himself unsteadily. He can see that the torches in the hall have been relit. No one is paying the two of them any particular attention, but Bran knows that won't last. His pain is dulled now. He feels battered, true, but the wound is closed and the councillor's dark magic no longer rends his flesh. Quickly he retrieves his weapons. At his feet is the dead councillor, his head split open. Bran looks at his father's blood-wet blades. Though he is ashamed to have been beaten by his enemy, he is filled with a fierce pride for his father's skills. Surely the O'Neal is the greatest warrior in the land.

Bran follows his father through the long halls of Loguire's mountain hold. The two ignore the questions flung at them by the confused people they pass, and those who try to stop them are met by the flashing blades of the O'Neals.

Section 4

Quickly they pass through the front gates where a handful of their retainers wait with saddled horses. Bran leaps up on his mount even as his father does the same.

"Father," he says, "what does this mean?" Rory looks at his son. Whirling his swords above his head to signal the others forward, he kicks his horse into a gallop. As Bran follows suit, his father cries above the pounding hoof beats.

"It means base treachery, my son, that and more. Treachery and red-handed war."

Rory has healed Bran. Give Bran 2 D6 hit points.

Turn to section 4.

Turn to section 4.

* **4** *

Return to Bran his original number of hit points. He has been healed in the time it has taken the O'Neals to reach their castle.

Bran jerks his horse to a halt and gazes at the castle before him. The sight of it has always filled him with exhilaration and a bit of trepidation. It stands on a high hill nestled among mountains. The town spread beneath its towering walls is well ordered and clean; the roofs of the buildings are painted in a pleasing variety of colors ranging from bright blue to deep maroon. The cobblestone streets are full of happy and prosperous people. But it is the castle that captures all of Bran's attention: Castle O'Neal. Home of the O'Neals for years uncounted. Its grey smooth walls rear up to fantastic heights as if to dare some invader to try to breach them. Its towers stand tall and straight like monuments to bravery and heroic deeds. And from each tower the banner of the O'Neals snaps in the wind. Two silver swords crossed, on a black field.

Bran wipes sweat from his eyes. Will this castle fall? Has the grand tale of the O'Neals finally come to an end? The young warrior is full of misgivings. His father has grown quieter in the last hours, brooding on the events at Loguire's hold. If only Sean were here, Bran thinks. But Sean is not. He disappeared in the western mountains five years ago when the King fought the rebel lords there. And with Sean gone, Bran is the last of the O'Neal's children, the heir to the castle and all that goes with it. His worst fears have come true.

The townspeople meet the approaching riders with cheers and glad cries, for they are glad to have their lord back among them. For hundreds of years the O'Neal clan has been known as the fiercest of all the lords of Gramarye. Yet they treat their people with respect and all know that here in their land are the best opportunities for the underclass. A man can rise far under the

benign rule of the O'Neals. That reason, even more than the fighting skills of the O'Neals, has made the clan prosperous. And when measured in men-at-arms, Sir Rory O'Neal's strength is more that of an earl than a baronet.

Bran turns his eyes from the adoring crowd on the road to the castle. He is unnerved by all the attention. He has been brought up as a second son and though his fighting skills—assisted by his magical powers—are superior to all but a few in the land of Gramarye, still he is unsure of himself. His father claims that civil war is coming and declares that the O'Neals will fight for the Queen. But Bran grinds his teeth at the thought of his family's castle under siege. They are so far away from the Queen's forces. Bran sighs. He must take the place of his brother and become Warleader, but how can he? In his heart he feels both he and his people are doomed.

That night a page brings him a summons from his father. Bran shakes his head. He knows what is coming. During the evening meal none spoke of the events at the duke's castle. But now plans must be made. And Bran must play his role as heir. Quietly he follows the page.

The page brings him to his father's workroom. Rory is already there with Elisabeth. Bran is not surprised to find his mother here; she has always had a hand in running the clan. She is still beautiful, despite her age; her bones are fine and strong, and the white hair on her head is thick and full and in its own way as beautiful as the gold of her youth. She holds out her arms to him and he kisses her dutifully, but he cannot raise his eyes to meet his father's gaze. Bran slips into a chair to face the two across the expanse of the oaken table. His eyes stray to the books which fill the shelf at the far end of the room.

"Bran," his father says, "Bran, we must prepare." The young warrior nods and turns toward his father. He is shocked by Rory's face. The years weigh heavy on the old warrior. For the first time Bran sees his father as a person, someone who must pay tribute to time's sad temple.

"I . . . I know, father," he answers, but his heart is far away.

"Your mother and I have been thinking." The old man shakes his head. "Since, since Sean's fall," Rory's voice breaks as he names his elder son. He tries again, "I meant to say that things do not go well for the country or for the O'Neals."

"I know, Father, that I am not worthy to replace my brother." Rory slams the table with his fist and Bran is shocked by his father's anger.

"That is not what I said, boy!" Rory shouts. "No one but yourself feels that way." But Bran does not answer and Rory shrugs hopelessly and turns to Elisabeth.

"Bran"—his mother's voice is calm—"Bran, no one accuses you of being less than your brother." Bran starts to say something but she silences him with a wave of her long-fingered hands. "No, we know you loved your brother well and truly and we all miss him." She takes a deep breath. "But, Bran, not only did we lose Sean, but with him we lost the Reaper."

"The Reaper," Bran repeats the name to himself. The sword of the O'Neals, the magic weapon that has been in his family since the first O'Neal. It never occurred to him, but Sean carried it with him to the wars, and when Sean was lost so was the Reaper.

"Yes, Mother," he says, "but what has that to do with the war?"

"Much," his father answers. "The Reaper is the sign of the O'Neals, the soul of our clan." The old man's eyes go bright as he remembers. "Forged of metals unknown to Gramarye, balanced like no other blade, thin, light, yes, but also stronger than any other blade in the world."

He turns to his son. "Bran, you know the strength of the O'Neals rests on our fighting skills, the martial form our dead ancestor developed."

Of course I know, Bran thinks. The whole land knows. The double-sword attack of the O'Neals is feared by all. From birth all the males of the O'Neal direct line are taught its use, along with the accompanying skills. Bran knows that he is nearly as deadly empty-handed as with his two blades.

"Yes, Father," he says, "but I still fail to see—" But Rory interrupts him again.

"Bran, the power of our clan has ever been the people and their fierce loyalty to us. Part of the loyalty comes from respect, respect for the

Section 4

O'Neal traditions and skills as well as for our generosity."

"The people are superstitious, Bran," Elisabeth adds. "They know there is more behind the O'Neal reputation than just a fancy fighting form. They know there is a magic to us." Bran frowns. His mother is a witch, but that knowledge is well hidden from the people, and he and his brother were given some small skill in the magical arts, but that too is not generally know. He shakes his head again. He still doesn't understand his parents' plan.

"The people love Catharine," Rory says. "They will fight for her, but," he adds, "we are far from the Queen. We must hold the castle and the lands about it. To do that we need the people strong and loyal to us."

"And," Elisabeth adds, "they all know the Reaper has been lost." She stares at her son for a moment. Slowly Bran begins to understand. Of course. Without the sword the superstitious will feel that the O'Neals are less than they were. Their very banner has the Reaper on it. Without the sword many would doubt that the O'Neals are strong, and suspect that God has somehow turned from them.

"If we are beaten on the battlefield, son," Rory continues, "then the enemy must besiege us. To besiege us they need sappers and miners, well stocked with supplies—need I go on?" The question is rhetorical. Bran understands now. Castle

O'Neal has never been taken. A stronghold such as the castle cannot be taken in assault; it must be taken in siege. And for a siege to work, many peasants and laborers are needed. Whenever this was tried in the past, the laborers hindered, not helped, the assault. For none of the underclass in the land wished to see the O'Neals' fall. The O'Neals never turned away those who came to them for protection from an unjust master, and the peasants depend not only on the justice of the O'Neals but in the O'Neals' strength to win against their enemies. After all, if they help the clan and the clan falls in spite of their aid, the peasants will pay a heavy price for their loyalty.

"There are rumors that the poor will make an army to fight for Catharine. All know we are loyal to our good Queen." Bran shakes his head in understanding. For the O'Neals to survive they need not only their own to be loyal, but for others to join them.

"We need a symbol to show that the O'Neals are still strong," Bran says.

"Exactly." Rory claps his hands together. "I can lead the war party, but you, my son, you must find the O'Neals' strength so that we may once again defy our enemies. Bring back the Reaper." Bran leaps to his feet. This is a task he can accomplish.

"I will, Father. I shall not fail." And his parents smile at the young warrior's confidence.

That long night the little family stays in the

study. Together they plan for the defense of the O'Neal lands and prepare for Bran's quest. The three pore over maps of the mountains and Bran memorizes the paths that lead to where his brother was last heard from: paths he must now retrace if he hopes to retrieve the weapon lost five long years ago. But though they study Sean's last trail, his name is carefully avoided, for none wish to bring up old grief for a well-loved brother and son. If Sean were alive his mother's magic would have found him long ago or Sean would have returned, the Reaper in his hand, laughing that they should have worried for his safety.

Bran knows, though none say as much to him, that privately his parents hope he can retrieve his brother's bones so that they might be properly buried. But even that hope is overshadowed by the larger issue. The Reaper must be found!

The next morning Bran leaves the castle. Though he has slept little, he is not tired. His quest beckons him on. He rides out by a back way, his father and mother's blessing still lingering in his mind. Underneath his cloak he wears the magic chainmail of his clan. This armor is the last of the great talismans of his family. It is a measure of his parents' faith in him that they gave it to him for this quest. For if he fails, then sword and armor and heir would all be lost and surely the O'Neals would be doomed.

His mother wished him to take companions, but both his father and Bran disagreed. All of the warriors will be needed for the castle's defense. Besides, one man can sneak into places that even five would be too many for. Bran is on his own, and that is how he has always preferred it.

It takes three days for Bran to reach the mountains and during that time he avoids all dwellings he chances near. But still he has felt the restlessness about him as the whole land moves toward an uncertain future. The war is coming and what will it leave in its wake?

Bran follows a cart trail toward a dark woods ahead. The woods spread out about the mountains' feet; it is on this path that his brother was last seen. As he approaches the woods he hears cries ahead. Urging his horse forward, he rounds a bend. On the road lie two overturned carts. Several peasants are running toward him. There are three bandits behind them, their weapons already red from those they have slain. Without thinking Bran draws his weapons and with a cry of "O'Neal!" he spurs his horse on toward the murderers.

BANDITS
To hit Bran: 14   To be hit: 13   Hit points: 5
Damage with pike: 1 D6−1 Damage with swords: 1 D6+2

Bran's chainmail subtracts 2 from any enemy's chance to hit him with weapons. As long as he retains the chainmail he gets this bonus.

Section 5

If Bran wins the fight turn to section 8.

If Bran loses the fight turn to section 9.

* **5** *

Bran wakes up abruptly. His body is sore, but he is alive. He sits up. He is under the shade of a tree that rises above him. About two hundred yards away he can see the road. There is only one cart there. He hears a noise behind him, and ignoring his stiffness, he spins and draws his weapon in one fluid motion. Facing him is the woman who healed him.

Bran can see she is not as old as he thought, perhaps in her late thirties, maybe even younger. Her appearance of age is due mainly to her silver-streaked hair and the lines that too much anguish has etched into her features. Her smile is gentle, but her eyes are full of things she finds hard to forget.

"The others are gone." Her voice is soft. "They have buried Paul and the others." Bran realizes she is talking about the men the bandits —no, soldiers—killed.

"Why did the soldiers attack you?"

"I don't know. I think, I think it was for fun." Her voice goes flat on the last word.

"Fun," Bran spits. "I regret that I did not come sooner."

"You came, you helped." The woman presses him to sit, then places a hand on his brow. "They would have killed us all if it hadn't been for you."

"I take it—" Bran turns away, his face already red—why was it always so hard for him to talk to people? "I take it I have you to thank for healing my wounds?" The words come out harder than he meant them to.

"I am a healer," she says simply, ignoring his discomfort.

"Some would say a witch." Again, Bran's words are harsher than he means.

"Perhaps, but many have the blood of witches in them, do they not, Bran O'Neal?" Bran can't help smiling at the woman. "Maybe some witches aren't what people think they are. Maybe there are good and bad witches as there are good and bad people."

"Maybe, lady, but I think it is an idea whose wisdom it is better not to test." The woman laughs and Bran smiles again at that gentle sound. Then he remembers his quest.

"Lady, do you know who these men were?" She grows serious at his question.

"Soldiers of one of the mountain lords," she answers. "Not all of those who rebelled five years ago were conquered, and now, now they join the other traitors in fighting our good queen Catharine." Bran nods. It was doubtful then that these soldiers were there specifically to attack him. Many would recognize the youngest O'Neal and it made sense that rebels would wish him dead, even if they did not know of his quest.

"Tell me, lady, were you here during the old wars?"

"No, I am newly come from the other side of the mountains, but as I understand it the fiercest fighting took place there." She points toward the forest at the foot of the mountains. "In there the battles raged day after day, and many of the fallen still rot in unknown groves and hollows." Bran feels a thrill. Yes, the fiercest fighting—that was where Sean would have been for sure, and if not all the dead have been recovered, then there is still a chance that his brother's remains can be found along with the Reaper.

"What do you know of this area?" he asks. The woman shrugs.

"Little, except that the woods here and the mountains are haunted by many things. I have myself seen signs of the little people, and darker creatures." Bran considers this awhile. He is not afraid, and while there is evil in these woods, still there might be those who would help him on his quest as this good woman has.

"Lady, is there nothing I can do to repay you for your kindness?" he says, remembering his chivalry.

"Have you not given me my life, young knight?" she answers, but there is a harshness in her voice. "My life," she says again softly, "my life without Paul." Before Bran can say anything the woman turns from him and picks up her small bundle of possessions.

"I must go. I must follow the others." She stares down at him, biting her lip. "There is said to be a witch in those woods," she says with a bitter smile, "a white witch, one who may help you. I do not know if this is true, but there are many more of us than most people suspect. Is that not so, Bran O'Neal?" Before he can answer, she walks away. Bran watches her dwindle in the distance, his own shyness keeping him from offering her help, or trying to get more information from her. With a shrug he sheaths his weapons and walks to the road.

There his horse lies dead. Some kind soul has released the animal from its misery. The three soldiers have been stripped of their weapons and armor and piled in the road beside a cart full of rags and such. And there are three new graves at the side of the road. Civil war is certainly the cruelest of man's inventions.

Quickly he removes his pack from his horse. Nothing has been touched. Lifting the ungainly burden onto his shoulders, he trudges down the road toward the waiting forest.

For the next hour Bran follows the path. The trees around him are getting larger and more numerous; off the path the undergrowth is very dense. But for all that, the forest is strangely quiet, as if it is holding its breath. The air is still, like it is before a rainstorm, but there are no clouds in the sky. Every once in a while an odd crackling can be heard as if some strange creature keeps pace with Bran. But he can sense nothing.

Finally he comes to a large standing stone. Here the road branches in three different directions. One leads off to Bran's right; it seems well used and he can see the cart tracks made by the peasants he has saved. At least he assumes it was the same cart. That path leads straight toward the mountains.

The second way leads straight on. It is overgrown and looks more like an animal trail. Bran sniffs the wind—water—he can smell it. This path must lead to a stream or a river. The animals of the forest probably use this way as a path to the water.

The third way leads off to the left. Obviously, it continues deeper into the woods. It, too, overgrown and seldom traveled, though it is much wider than the second trail. Which way should he go?

If he heads toward the mountains he will be heading toward the strongholds of the warlords, the same folk that his brother was fighting. If he heads toward the water, well, if he wants to find the white witch she will most likely be near the water and she might have information he can use. The third path leads deeper into the woods, and the healer told him that these woods were the site of much of the fiercest fighting in the old war. If he is to find his brother it will most likely be along that path.

If Bran should take the first path, toward the mountains, turn to section 10.

If he should take the second path, toward the water, turn to section 6.

If he should take the third path, deeper into the woods, turn to section 14.

* **6** *

Bran follows the path for a few hours, eating his meal as he walks. The forest is stifling, as if it watches him and is weighing whether he belongs here or not. He sees no sign of life anywhere—no animals, no birds, and certainly no people.

The path slowly gets rougher and becomes little more than a trail. The sound of running water is getting stronger with every step he takes. Occasionally he hears scrambling by the path, but neither his magic nor his martial abilities can detect anything. Still, he has a strange feeling that he is being followed.

As Bran crests a small hill he is confronted with the sight of a raging river not ten miles away. The path turns to follow the path of the water. He shrugs to himself and continues on the way.

The river is loud as it tears among the rapids but it is still the only sound in the forest. The fact that the only sound comes from the water makes it strangely threatening and Bran finds himself watching the water with a cautious eye.

The path along here seems better traveled and it turns abruptly away from the river and plunges back into the forest. The hairs on the back of Bran's neck rise. Something is wrong, but what? Suddenly he comes out of the woods into a clearing which holds an apparently empty thatched hut.

Bran stops and studies it warily. From above him a voice cries out in a high-pitched whine.

"State your name, warrior, and your purpose in intruding upon me."

Bran whirls toward the voice, drawing his weapons, but he can see nothing. Looking above him he sees a black crow regarding him with bloodshot eyes.

"My name is Bran O'Neal, and my purposes are my own," he answers, a little chagrined at talking to a bird.

"O'Neal," the voice answers, though the bird's beak does not move. "O'Neal, well, your name is known here, lad, and members of your family are always welcome. Turn and face me." Bran spins about and there, not ten feet away, stands a woman. She is in her sixties at least. Her face is creased with wrinkles, and her hair lies about her shoulders like grey moss. But she holds herself erect, and her eyes are black and strong.

"I am Reagon." She holds her hand out and the crow flies to it, fixing Bran with the same unfriendly gaze. "And this is Corvus." The crow stretches its neck out and clacks its beak at Bran. "Don't mind him; he is a rather rude creature." The bird cocks its head in agreement.

"Madam," Bran says, but again his shyness makes his words stumble, "I didn't come to, uh, I mean I didn't know you lived here. I didn't think anyone lived in this nasty forest."

"Indeed." Reagon cocks her eyebrows at that. "Nasty forest is it?" but she smiles to see Bran's answering blush.

"Sit, lad." Reagon's voice is still weirdly high-pitched, but not unfriendly. "Sit and tell me what has brought you to this 'nasty' forest." Bran crouches across from the woman and tells her of his search for his brother's remains, though he makes no mention of the Reaper. The whole way through, the woman and bird stand there silent and unmoving. There is a pause when Bran finishes. The woman nods her head once.

"Well, you have not told me the whole reason for your visit," she says. Bran starts to disagree, but she stops him with an upraised hand. "Now, Bran O'Neal, don't bother with that. I don't think you'd make a very good liar."

"I can see your full reasons are more important than those you state. Otherwise, why would a fine strapping warrior such as yourself be here instead of preparing for the war to come?" Bran says nothing. "Well, you have your reasons for your silence, I'm sure. So I will help you." Bran's face lights with eagerness.

"First, I know nothing of your brother, but I might be able to help you in other ways." The woman points to a small vial almost hidden in the moss at her feet. "This is an ointment, one that takes a long year to create." Bran stares at it in fascination.

"What's in it?"

"Witch-moss for one, water, nothing dangerous. Take it," she says. "If rubbed on wounds, such as a warrior is bound to acquire in this place, it will help them to heal faster. There is only sufficient for one wound but used wisely, it could save your life." Bran picks up the vial and thanks her profusely, but she reacts not at all.

"Now a little wisdom. You shall not find what you seek in this woods. The mountains are where you must go, and these mountains are the most dangerous place in all of Gramarye. Past my home"—she points at the house behind her—"the path breaks. One way leads you straight to the mountains, the quickest route; that is to your right. The second leads to danger and perhaps the first of your answers. That way is to your left. And the last thing I will tell you, Bran O'Neal, is that this woods is silent for fear, and I think the answers you seek will only be found in confronting that fear." With that the woman and bird waver like an image on water, then they and the house behind them are gone.

Bran leaps to his feet with a start. What does this mean? He holds the potion vial in his hand judiciously. Unstoppering it carefully, he takes a tiny bit of the liquid on his finger, then rubs it on a scratch on his arm. First there is great heat and Bran fears he has been betrayed, but then the scratch heals itself in moments. Whoever the woman was, she obviously meant him no harm.

Sheathing his weapons Bran continues on the path. He comes to the break in it. Which way? Toward danger and a possible answer? Or straight toward the mountains and what the woman called his ultimate destination?

Add the healing potion to Bran's possessions. It may be used once to cure 1 D6 worth of injuries.

If Bran decides to go straight toward the mountains, turn to section 17.

If Bran decides to head toward the unknown danger, turn to section 19.

* **7** *

The troll's first blow misses Bran, smashing into the earth where he stood moments before. The skull is smashed into a thousand splinters. Before the monster can recover, Bran slashes it across its left leg with his long sword. Thick red blood slowly leaks from the wound, but the creature does not seem to notice.

Again and again its great club slashes at Bran; time and again he ducks under the blow or nimbly avoids it. His weapons reach out to cut the monster on its legs, its chest, its back, but still the creature attacks, its bellows of outrage nearly deafening the young warrior.

Bran knows that if the troll manages to hit him, he is a dead man. The power in the creature's arm is unbelievable. Bran is nearly caught when one of the creature's wild blows slams into a young pine, breaking it like a twig and nearly trapping Bran beneath the tree as it falls. Bran ducks in, out, cuts, slashes, dives, rolls. He calls up every trick he has, whether martial or magical, to use against the monster. And still it will not die.

Finally Bran is backed against another tree. He is tired and bruised and the monster has come close to killing him more than once. He watches as the ponderous creature approaches. Then his eyes fasten on a tree limb a few feet above the trail. Here is his chance.

As the creature swings again, Bran lets go of his short sword and leaps to catch hold of the limb. Even as the troll's club smashes into the tree, Bran swings himself up into the air and over the head of the monster. Before the troll can turn to reach Bran, he regains his feet and grasping his long sword in two hands, he slashes through the monster's back, severing its spine and bursting its black heart.

Bran stands over his dead foe, his breath coming in painful heaves. He withdraws his sword and meticulously wipes the thick gore off it. Retrieving his short sword he looks down at the troll once more. He shakes his head, how could it be? He was half witch, but never, never did he truly believe such monsters as this existed. Where had it come from? He spits on the ground, resheaths his weapons, and continues grimly on his path.

Record any hit points Bran has lost.

Turn to section 15.

* **8** *

Bran quickly takes in the situation even as he urges his horse to charge. Near the two over-turned carts are three bodies. Two of the bandits are standing over them, swords wet with the blood of their victims. Coming straight at Bran are four women and five children. The peasants leap from the road to avoid Bran's horse.

Standing behind them, directly in Bran's path, is the third bandit. He is a big man. A heavy chainmail shirt hangs from his wide shoulders. He holds a gleaming pike. As he rides past, Bran reaches across his horse's neck and deflects the bandit's swing with the pike. The shock of the blow nearly unhorses him, but he grimly holds on. He spins his horse to charge again.

The horse rears, gives an almost human scream of pain, and falls to the ground. Bran barely has time to leap from the animal before it can crush him. Quickly he is back on his feet. Now all three of the bandits are facing him from across the form of his thrashing horse.

This makes no sense. The bandits should have run away when they saw the young knight charge. Their kind always does. Bran takes in their chainmail and weapons, all well cared for and well made. He turns to his horse quickly. Now he understands. The animal has been hamstrung by the bandit with the pike. It takes long years of training to master that technique. These are not bandits. They are soldiers, disguised. Why?

"Who are you?" he shouts. "Who is your lord? Why do you attack these people?"

"We know you," the big one answers. "We know you, Bran O'Neal, and high is the price placed on your head." The three move closer. "Give up now boy, or we'll kill you where you stand."

"Give up!" Bran's voice is incredulous. "I am an O'Neal." With that he charges. His two swords whirl before him. The soldiers seek to surround him, but he is too quick for them. He dives among them, never exposing his back. Twice his chainmail saves him. More times than can be counted, one of his swords stops a blade inches from his body.

The first of the soldiers goes down when Bran's short sword pierces the man's mail under the arm. The second falls moments later as Bran's other sword cuts him across the throat. Then there is only the pike man left.

"Die, traitor," Bran hisses as the soldier drops his pike and draws his sword. They charge one another and crash together like two great bulls. The soldier hides a poignard in his left hand and nearly takes Bran's life with it. But the young knight is too quick. He deflects the thrust with his elbow and slices down with his short sword, nearly severing his enemy's head.

It is over in moments. Bran stands over the

corpses, breathing hard. He is covered in bruises and cuts that he never even felt in the heat of battle.

The peasant women approach him carefully, their eyes red with the unshed tears for their dead men. The eldest reaches toward Bran as if in supplication.

"I am a healer, master. Let me tend to you."

"No, Molly," one of the others cries, "you must not."

"Quiet," the healer answers. "This man has saved our lives. I do not think he is the type to burn as a witch an old woman who wishes to repay his gallantry."

"Thank you, lady." Bran's voice is quiet as his natural shyness comes back. "I, I would never turn on any who befriend me." The woman smiles and as her hands touch Bran's head he feels a great warmth race through his veins. He collapses.

"Yes, lad"—the woman's voice is all he can focus on—"you would not turn on one of your own, would you?" And with that Bran loses consciousness.

The healer will bring Bran back to full hit points. Return these to their original number on your record sheet before continuing.

Turn to section 5.

* **9** *

Bran quickly surveys the situation even as he urges his horse to charge. Near the two overturned carts are three bodies. Two of the bandits are standing over the corpses, their swords wet with the blood of their victims. Coming straight toward Bran are four women and five children. The peasants jump from the road to avoid Bran's horse.

Standing directly in Bran's path is the third bandit. He is a big man, a heavy chainmail shirt hangs from his wide shoulders. He holds a gleaming pike. Bran reaches across his horse's neck and deflects the bandit's swing with the pike. The shock of the blow nearly unhorses Bran, but he grimly holds on. He spins his horse to charge again.

The horse rears, gives an almost human scream of pain, then falls to the ground. Bran barely has time to leap from the animal before it can crush him. Quickly he is back on his feet. Now all three of the bandits are facing him from across the body of his still thrashing horse.

This makes no sense. The bandits should have run away when they saw the young knight charge; their kind always does. He glances at his horse. It has been hamstrung—a lucky stroke? Such a technique is hard-learned. Few warriors could pull it off. What sort of bandits are these?

"Who are you?" he shouts. "Why did you attack these people?"

"We know you," the big one answers. "We know you, Bran O'Neal, and high is the price placed on your head." The three move closer. Now Bran understands. The rebel lords must have put a bounty on him. The thought of the money was making the bandits brave.

"Give up, boy, or we will kill you where you stand," the big one shouts.

"Give up!" Bran's voice is incredulous. "I am an O'Neal." With that he charges. His swords whirl before him. The bandits seek to surround Bran, but he is too quick for that. He dives among them, never exposing his back. Twice his chainmail saves him. More times than can be counted, one of his swords stops a blade inches from his body.

The first of the soldiers goes down with a bad cut across his shoulder. Bran cannot tell if the wound is mortal or not. The second falls moments later when Bran's long sword catches him deep in the thigh. Then there is only the pike man facing him.

"Die, traitor," Bran hisses as the bandit drops his pike and draws his sword. For a moment Bran is surprised. The bandit's sword is a well-made and costly weapon. Where could a bandit have gotten such a prize? The bandit charges him and crashes into Bran like a bull. Bran parries his enemy's sword, but he feels a sharp stab in his side. Even as he crashes to the ground he stares unbelievingly at the poignard sticking from him. How could it be—Bran O'Neal bested by bandits? The bandit stands over him, his blade raised to sever Bran's head. And then, too late, Bran realizes his mistake. These are no bandits but hardened warriors, warriors sent to kill him.

He hears a cry above him, and the man is replaced by a woman, a woman holding a blood-reddened pike. She throws the weapon away with distaste and bends down close to Bran.

"You are safe now, young one," she whispers in his ear, but Bran knows his wounds are mortal. He has failed, and his clan will die with him.

"No, no," the woman says as if she can read his mind. "I am a healer. I will save you." But Bran cannot understand her words as the whole world goes dark, and only a strong echo of sound can be heard, an echo of one word. "Fail, fail, fail."

The healer brings Bran back to half his hit points. His chainmail has been damaged and now only gives him A +1 bonus. Note this on your record sheet.

Turn to section 5.

* **10** *

Well, this is probably the best way, Bran thinks to himself. His brother was last seen entering these mountains with twenty men. He was probably planning to raid some mountain lord's keep. Bran knows it is in the mountains that he will find the answers to his quest.

The path slowly begins to get rockier. Bran can still see the cart tracks, but he can't tell if the soldiers came this way or not. After a few miles the path begins to get steeper. Bran takes a few moments to make a quick meal, then heads determinedly on.

The stillness of the forest is beginning to get to him; surely at least a bird should cry out. Whatever has been following him, if anything has, is gone now. It feels as if Bran were the only living thing for a hundred miles. The path branches off again. The tracks of the cart lead off to Bran's left, but what's the use of following them? No, it's straight ahead, straight into the heart of these accursed mountains.

The woods begin to thin out, oaks giving way to pine. But still no sight or sound of life. Bran stumbles over something. Reaching down he picks up the object and examines it.

A skull! A human skull, and something has crushed the crown of it. Bran looks at it closer, running his fingers along the rift at the top. No, he thinks, not crushed, but bitten. God, what could bite through the skull of a man? Then with a sob Bran catches himself—is this his brother? He drops the skull at his feet.

"Oh, God," he cries, "oh, God, Sean. Is this your end?" Nothing answers the young warrior's cry. He leans down to examine the skull more closely. He can see now that it could not be Sean, for the jaw was outslung; whoever had such a jaw would have had a terrible underbite. No, it isn't Sean, but who is it, and, he shudders, what killed him?

Suddenly a shadow covers Bran and he looks up to a horrid sight.

There, standing before him, is a creature at least eight feet tall. It is vaguely human but massively deformed: one arm withered and useless, the other thick and obscenely muscled. Clutched in that terrible arm is a thick stone club with jagged edges. The creature's skin is tough and covered with patches of different color hide. It wears an old wolf pelt as a loin cloth. Its thick, tree-stump legs are hairy like an animal's. But it is its face that is truly horrifying.

Its head is oblong and forms into a small snout where two great canines surrounded by pointed brown teeth glare at him in a parody of a smile. The face is patched and quilted in reds and browns as if someone had sewn skin on it from fifty different animals. And its eyes are yellow.

"Manfood," it hisses, "manfood," and it raises

Section 11

its club above its head. Bran draws his swords. A troll, he thinks, good God, a troll, and with that he prepares to fight for his life.

TROLL
*To hit Bran: 10   To be hit: 14   Hit Points: 18
Damage with club: 1 D6   Damage with swords: 1 D6+2*

If Bran wins the fight with the troll, turn to section 7.

If Bran loses the fight with the troll, turn to section 90.

* **11** *

This is a fool's game, Bran decides. Even if he could kill the monster, what end would it serve? Wherever the creature's lair lies, it would have to be underwater, and there's no way Bran is going to risk swimming in this water.

The creature keeps moving toward Bran, snapping its jaws in anticipation. Certes, Bran thinks, this thing is not going to offer any help to my search. The beast wants to devour me. Having decided that there is no point in continuing this fight, Bran turns and runs into the woods.

It takes him a while to find the path again, and this time he makes sure to stay away from the river. When he finds another path that leads toward the mountains, he follows that. As far as Bran's concerned, the sooner he gets out of these woods the better.

The new trail takes him to a shallow place in the river. Here the water seems more normal. Bran studies the currents for a while and judges the place passable. He takes a deep breath. "Discretion is the better part of valor," he says aloud as he crosses the ford at a full run. He doesn't stop running until the river is lost from view behind him.

Bran continues toward the mountains. He is out of the forest now. The area is rocky and the path is getting steeper. After a long climb he stops and rests among the jumbled rocks.

Well, he thinks to himself, in the ballads the heroes never turn back. Then again, in the ballads the heroes generally get killed, don't they? And he laughs softly. The sound echoes weirdly in the empty place, but Bran can't help himself. After a long while he quiets down, but the laughing continues.

At least it sounds like laughing, but not human laughing. He scrambles to the top of the nearest rise. There is a wisp of smoke rising above a stand of trees in the small valley just in front of him. The laughing is coming from there and now that he's closer it seems to have an evil sound.

As he worms his way through the brush at the bottom of the valley, he can hear the sound more clearly and the source is finally in view. There are several creatures and all are making the same strange sound. Then he hears another voice.

"Help! Gods preserve me, get these nasty creatures from—ah, go on . . . vermin." At least that's what it sounds like. Well, someone is in trouble; Bran can tell that. Bran cannot abandon a person in need. He draws his blade.

Turn to section 16.

* **12** *

The path becomes even harder to see. No sound comes from anywhere around and Bran begins to worry if perhaps he is the only living creature in this part of the forest. To make it all even more annoying, Bran can tell that the path is again veering toward the mountains.

Still he moves stealthily. The woods are thinning now, and pines replace the oaks of the forest. The undergrowth is becoming thin in places and the path is rocky and overgrown. Bran realizes he is already in the foothills and is despairing of finding any answers before he reaches the mountains. Then he sees a small wisp of smoke ahead of him. Someone's here, he thinks, and whoever it is is about to get a visitor, welcome or not.

He moves across the rough rocky terrain easily and quietly, crosses over a ridge and looks down at a small valley. That is where the smoke is coming from. He moves closer to investigate.

As he nears the middle of a small patch of wood Bran hears a strange sound. It is laughter, but a wicked laughter. And there is something else; someone is yelling and cursing. Bran can't quite make out the words, but he isn't stupid. Obviously someone is in trouble and they need help, fast.

He draws his swords and moves quietly through the thin undergrowth toward the voice.

Turn to section 16.

* **13** *

The second Bran breaks from cover the gremlins are aware of him. Their laughter forgotten, they turn to face the intruder with horrible cries. There are eight of the little creatures. Four turn to rush Bran while the others gather in a little group away from the fire. Fighting the monsters is more difficult than Bran thought it would be. The gremlins are inhumanly fast. They leap and dive about like so many wasps. They leap for his throat and grab hold of his arms and legs to try to trip him up. Bran's swords don't frighten the monsters.

But for all their viciousness the gremlins are not very sturdy, and when Bran's blows do connect, the creatures are easily killed. Bran tries to get close enough to help the little man tied over the fire, but his attackers keep him back. Bran's swords flash and another of the gremlins falls. But one is still left, and four haven't even attacked yet.

Bran steals a look at the others. They have formed a circle, holding hands, dancing in time to a weird chant which is unlike any Bran has heard before. But Bran is aware of his danger: this is magic. With a shout he throws off his last attacker and charges straight at the chanting gremlins. They break their circle and turn to face him. As they turn a bright light flashes from the ground where they danced, and Bran is hit in the chest.

The force of the blow knocks him off his feet, and he again feels the strange biting pain that the councillor's knife had assailed him with. While he is stunned the four return to their dance and renew their chant while the fifth gremlin leaps on Bran's shoulders and tries to bury its fangs in his throat.

Bran doubts he can withstand another of their magical attacks and has only seconds to act before the creatures' magic can strike him again. He drops his short sword and grabs the vicious creature. With a convulsive surge of strength he crushes the little monster. Leaping to his feet Bran dives among the others, breaking their circle again.

The gremlins' magic is dissipated, and before

the creatures can reorganize, Bran attacks them with the speed of a whirlwind. In moments the battle is all over. His foes dead, Bran turns to help their victim. But the little man is no longer hanging from the fire. He sits with his back to Bran, roasting something over the fire.

Turn to section 25.

* **14** *

Bran follows the path into the woods for several hours and he begins to doubt the wisdom of his choice. There are no signs of any creatures along the path, and it seems to be just a meandering, random trail, with no destination in sight. He eats a hasty meal as he walks.

The path becomes little more than a trail, and Bran is despondent over the thought of spending the night in this strange silent forest. As the area becomes hillier Bran realizes he is heading once more into the mountains. He feels like the very land about him is saying to him, "Well, you've seen the forest, nothing here, so why don't you get back to your quest and quit messing around?" Bran is beginning to think that's good advice. But just as he is about to turn from this path and head toward the mountains he spies something on the path.

It is a bone, a human bone, and it looks like

something has been gnawing on it recently. In the mud beside the bone is a footprint. It looks almost human, but it is huge, and at the end of each of its five toe marks is a slight indentation as if whatever had made that giant footprint had claws. Bran draws his swords silently; it seems he may not be the only one in the forest after all. Bran decides to investigate.

The prints finally lead Bran to a small cave. The cave smells terrible and yellowing bones are scattered all around it. Bran sifts through them carefully. Most are from animals, but some are human. All are gnawed and broken.

Bran examines the human bones, half afraid of what he might find. Is this the end that his brave brother met so many years ago? But no, he finds the discarded clothes of the dead men, and they are all in the colors of one of the mountain lords. Still, some of the bones here are years old. Could the creature that killed these men be the one that killed Sean?

There is nothing in the cave fit for human consumption and no further clues of what did all this killing. Outside the cave, the path continues, and a new one branches off toward the mountains. Bran thinks a moment. Should he continue the way he has gone? Perhaps it leads to something after all. Or maybe this creature, whatever it is, is some sort of guardian protecting the area. Or then again . . . he looks up at the snow-capped peaks of the mountains; the creature's footprints lead off in that direction. He thinks,

Should he follow them and hope to catch the monster and maybe get some idea of what is going on?

If Bran stays on the path he is on, turn to section 12.

If Bran should follow the monster's trail and head toward the mountains, turn to section 88.

* **15** *

The path now turns to the mountains. It climbs, but slowly, almost imperceptibly. The trail does not look as if it sees much use. Periodically, Bran finds more bones, both human and animal scattered about; all are cracked and look chewed.

Bran follows the path over a hill. From the top of the hill he can see a small valley and a thick stand of trees. There is a small wisp of smoke coming from the middle of the wooded area. He can hear something moving around down there. He moves closer cautiously.

As he enters the woods he hears strange cries that sound somewhat like laughter, but certainly not human laughter. And above that strange sound he hears another voice.

"Och, get your paws off me, ye greasy devils. Do you think you can get away with this, you bleedin' beasties? Ho, you'll rot for this, surely. Ye gods, where are you now when I need ya? Save

me, save me from these nasty beasties, save me!"
The voice becomes more frantic with each moment. Bran has no idea what's going on, but
someone is in danger, and he must see if he can
be of help.

Turn to section 16.

* **16** *

Bran moves through the undergrowth quickly,
but he is silent as only an O'Neal can be. He
comes to a halt as soon as he sees the orange light
of a fire ahead of him. Crawling on his stomach
he moves in for a closer look. It is truly a bizarre
sight.

Tiny figures surround the fire. They are naked
and covered with dull green scales and aren't
more than a foot tall. Their faces are like monkeys, but with sharp-looking teeth, and their
large, pointed ears are set on top of their heads.
The creatures are rolling around by the fire,
laughing their perverse laughter, and the object
of their glee is bound and hanging over the
flames.

It is one of the little people, his long white
beard already singed by the flames beneath him,
his little pot belly red from the heat. He's been
hung over the fire on a spit, like a hare, and he is

screaming at the top of his voice, not in fear but in pure anger.

"Ah, you damn green devils! Roast me, will ya? Well, the gods' black curse on you, you miserable excuse for monsters. Off with ya now or meet with my awesome rage!" All his threats seem to do is make his captors laugh the harder. Bran has to hide a smile himself. It all looks so ridiculous, but the little man is in real danger, and these creatures, whatever they are, are nothing to be laughed off.

Bran bursts from his cover and charges with a great cry of "O'Neal!"

GREMLINS
To hit Bran: 16   To be hit: 10   Hit points: 3
Damage with claws: 1 D6−3
Damage with swords: 1 D6+2

The gremlins have limited magic ability. As long as there are four left they can throw a lightning bolt at Bran. The bolt hits on a 12 and does 1 D6 of damage. There are eight gremlins.

If Bran wins the fight, turn to section 13.

If he loses, turn to section 21.

©1986

* **17** *

Bran takes the path to the right. Obviously there will be dangers enough for him in this quest—no point in looking for trouble. Besides, he's been told that whatever answer he will ultimately need can be found in the mountains. Resolutely he follows his chosen path.

The trail leads toward the river again. Finally it stops at a stone bridge. The water is quiet here, but as Bran crosses the bridge he finds himself watching the water nervously. It is so deep he cannot see the bottom, but somehow he knows that something is down there, something he does not wish to meet. Quickly he crosses the bridge and follows the trail on the other side.

The woods give way to scrub forest with little undergrowth. Bran continues on. Still, it is so silent and there is a terrible threat in that unnatural quiet.

Bran spots a strange pile of rocks ahead, to the left of the trail. As he moves closer he sees they are not rocks after all, but bones. Human bones.

He kneels down to inspect them. Handling them gently, he sees there are two skulls, several thigh bones, and numerous pieces of the spine. Is this the end of his quest? Does this place mark the sad end of Sean O'Neal?

Bran knows that all the bones are fairly recent. He picks them up and carefully examines each one individually though his breath comes in gasps. The bones have all been broken—no, not just broken but cracked and crushed, as if demolished by some tremendous force. Worst of all, some of the bones have been chewed, and quite recently, chewed by something with humongous teeth. Bran shudders. What does this mean?

He stands up and warily continues on his way, trying to guess what kind of creature could be responsible for that sad pile of bones.

Turn to section 15.

* **18** *

Bran moves back from the edge of the water slowly, to see if he can draw the monster out onto land. The strange head watches him intently and slowly and cautiously the creature lumbers out of the water after him.

It looks like a giant salamander with an elongated head and no tail. The monster is at least twenty feet from the tip of its head to its back legs. It stands about five feet high, with thick stumpy legs holding its belly only a few inches off the ground. The neck on the thing is at least ten feet long and is as flexible as a snake's. Its hue is a horrible mottled brown color which makes the creature look diseased. After his first smell of it, Bran takes another step back.

Whether meeting this monster will yield any answers to his quest does not matter now, for to rid the world of a water dragon is a worthy deed in itself. Bran's weight is balanced on his toes. This could be the greatest battle of his life.

WATER DRAGON
To hit Bran: 11   To be hit: 12   Hit points: 25
Damage with bite: 1 D6 − 1   Damage with sword:
1 D6 + 2

If Bran wins the fight, turn to section 20.

If Bran loses the fight, turn to section 89.

* **19** *

Bran takes the path to the left. He knows things can only get more dangerous on this quest, so why put off the inevitable? Besides, the witch woman, Reagon, mentioned the possibility of there being some clue in this direction to the answers he is seeking.

The path winds its way in a seemingly haphazard fashion. The forest is still uncannily quiet, though after a while Bran can hear the slow murmur of water ahead. After half an hour of walking, the trail veers toward the river. The water is moving slowly, as if it were somehow thicker than water should be. The path parallels the river and Bran continues along it, watching the water warily.

The river widens and its banks are no longer so sharply defined. It is full of small pools and treacherous mud. Abruptly the trail ends and Bran finds himself facing a swamp.

The place is dreary and grey. All the trees in this area look drained somehow, as if instead of the water giving the vegetation strength, it were sapping it. There is sound here, but it is the annoying buzz of hungry insects. Bran hears a noise from the water, as if someone had dropped a rock in thick mud.

He can see a strange ripple forming under the

water, a ripple of water that moves slowly, but steadily, straight toward him.

He draws his sword just as a large brown object lifts from the water. At first he thinks it is a branch, but then it undulates like a great snake. But even as Bran thinks that, he sees there is a small face at the end of the thing, a face full of teeth and with one bright yellow eye. Unconsciously, he steps back, nearly slipping in the mud.

The creature, whatever it is, is moving closer and still he stands, indecisive. Is this the danger, the danger that once met may yield answers to his quest? Or is this just a fool's errand he has been sent on? Did the witch just see this as a chance to get rid of a creature that threatened her? He still has time. He could run. He doubts that the monster could catch him on land.

If Bran decides to fight, then turn to section 18.

If Bran decides to run, turn to section 11.

* **20** *

The monster moves closer and Bran waits to learn its method of attack. The creature is now within ten feet of the warrior. Its gait, out of the water, is awkward and slow. But the head—Bran knows—is the danger.

Section 20

The creature hisses at him, revealing the rows of jagged teeth in its small snout. Then the head dips down with the speed of a lightning bolt. Bran avoids the teeth, but is bowled over when the creature whips its head back up, smacking Bran in the shoulder. Quickly the dragon attacks again, and again, and again.

Bran loses all conscious thought as he just reacts to his opponent's inhuman speed. His vision is filled with the snapping mouth and the one angry, soulless eye. Again and again Bran's swords cut deep into the creature's leather hide, but to little purpose. His blows seem only to enrage the dragon.

Bran is tiring fast, the footing is treacherous, but he must at all costs avoid the dragon's teeth. He sees a good example of how powerful those jaws are, when the dragon, missing Bran, snaps a chunk out of a tree in its rage. But Bran does see a chance. The creature, for all its speed, has poor aim, probably due to the fact that it has only one eye. More importantly, the neck, while incredibly flexible, has a limited range of movement. The creature can strike anything in front of it or to the side, but it seems unable to turn to protect itself against attacks from the rear.

Gambling everything on one move Bran dodges, and as the creature's head rears back up into striking position, Bran leaps past the jaws and right over the back of the creature. Immediately the dragon tries to turn around to face him but Bran is too quick.

Like a great cat he leaps onto the monster's back and his claws are deadly. He drives his short sword deep into the creature's spine. Using the securely embedded weapon as a hand-hold, he rides out the monster's futile attempts to dislodge him and strikes the snake's neck with his long sword. Over and over he cuts, till the neck is severed. For a few moments the head and the body do an odd dance of death. Then the body collapses, and the snake head moves no more.

Bran is hurt and tired, but a fierce thrill infuses him. He leaps up on the body of his dead enemy and cries: "O'Neal! O'Neal! O'Neal!" until the silent woods echo with his cry.

Bran tends his own wounds as best he can. Then he searches the creature's body but finds no clue. Its lair, he thinks. I must find its lair.

After nearly an hour of searching Bran finds a way across the swamp. Following the dragon's great claw prints he carefully picks his way through the muck and mire. At last he comes to a slime-caked bit of rock. He sees a small opening and carefully moves inside.

Besides a horrendous smell and some rotting bones, Bran can find nothing. So what is the clue he is supposed to find? All there is is the monster. That's it. The monster. None ever reported such a creature before. Certes, there are always stories, and there are monsters aplenty. But his mother has taught him that many are myths, and surely the creature he just fought could not be natural. The body of the dragon doesn't even fit together. It is as if someone has taken parts from different animals and bound them together. Is that it? Is the answer he seeks not in the monster but in its master?

Musing over the new questions this raises, Bran leaves the swamp and starts toward the mountains. Soon he stumbles upon a new path. Deciding that it's better to stick to a path than to wander around aimlessly, he follows it.

Soon it leads him deep into the woods again. The same quiet prevails here as did in the woods across the swamp. Grimly Bran continues on, but he moves more cautiously. If he's learned nothing else in his time here, he's learned that this place is very, very dangerous.

The path becomes little more than a trail. Bran wonders if there's any point in continuing to follow it? Shrugging his shoulders, he realizes he probably couldn't retrace his steps anyway. Whatever waits for him ahead, he will have to trust it will provide all the answers he needs.

Turn to section 12.

* **21** *

The second Bran breaks out of his cover the gremlins are aware of him. Their laughter forgotten, they turn to face the intruder with horrible cries. There are eight of the little creatures. Four turn to rush Bran while the others gather in a little group away from the fire. Fighting the monsters is more difficult than Bran thought it would be. The gremlins are inhumanly fast. They leap and dive about like so many wasps. They leap at his throat and arms, grab hold of his legs to try to trip him. Bran's swords don't seem to frighten the monsters.

But for all their viciousness the gremlins are not very sturdy, and when Bran's blows do connect, the creatures are easily killed. Bran tries to aid the little man tied over the fire, but his attackers keep him back. Bran's swords flash and another of the gremlins falls. But one of his original attackers is still left, and the other four haven't attacked yet.

Bran steals a look at the others. They have formed a circle, holding hands, dancing in time to a weird chant which is unlike any Bran has ever heard, but he is aware of his danger: this is magic. With a shout he throws off his attacker and charges straight at the chanting gremlins. They break their circle and turn to face him. As they do, a bright light flashes from the ground where they were dancing and hits Bran in the chest with some force.

The blow knocks him off his feet, and he feels the same strange biting pain that the councillor's knife had assailed him with. While he is stunned, the four return to their dance and renew their chant even as the fifth gremlin leaps on Bran's shoulders to try to bury its fangs in his throat.

Bran doubts he can withstand many of these magic attacks. He must stop the vicious creature at his throat before its companions' magic can strike him again. He drops his short sword and grabs the creature. With a convulsive surge of strength he crushes the little monster. Leaping to his feet Bran dives among the others, breaking their circle again.

But Bran is a moment too late, and again the strange magic shocks him. As he tries to recover from the last of the gremlins' attack he struggles to defend himself. Bran tries to hold on to consciousness, but he is weak from the magical blow, and suddenly he knows this is his day to die.

Even as he collapses, he hears a strange voice cry something. Moments pass and though Bran can no longer see, he can still hear.

"It's all right, lad, ye've done well. Just you rest a moment and you'll be fine."

Oddly enough Bran is beginning to feel better, and though he is still hurt, he manages to sit up a bit. He looks to the fire to see if the little man still lives and is startled to see that the gremlins' victim is no longer hanging over the fire. His back is to the warrior and he holds something else over the fire.

Give Bran back half his hit points as the little man has healed him. If Bran has met the witch, then cross off the healing potion (if he hasn't already used it) as the little man will use it to help heal the warrior.

Turn to section 25.

* **22** *

The tower is some thirty feet high. It is made of dressed stone. But the stone is strangely wet, as if it were sweating. Bran's feet continually slip as he climbs.

   Little by little, Bran pulls himself up, but it is slow work. As the rope picks up the moisture, it is getting more and more difficult to hold tight. Finally he manages to pull himself up to the window. He looks in, but it's so dark within that he can see nothing. Gingerly he pulls himself up on the rotting windowsill and starts to move inside. Suddenly something grips his shoulder. It is a small hand.

Turn to section 36.

* **23** *

"That's right," Neal continues, "the Reaper. Did I not say I was an O'Neal, too?"

"Yes, but—" Bran begins.

"Yes, but nothing," Neal interrupts. "This insurrection against Her Highness is unlawful and the little people will do what they can to help her majesty. My part is to keep the O'Neals a force to reckon with. And to do their part the clan needs the sword, now doesn't it?"

"Yes, but I mean . . ."

"Nah, nah, lad, you have the tongue of an ox. Don't you know that speaking is an art form?" Neal shakes his head in disgust. "Och, to think you, *you* are the heir to the O'Neals. Why, what is this world coming to?" Bran has no answer to that.

"Well now, lad, let me ask you now, have you found anything yet that could help us?"

"No, no, I guess not. This place is said to be where my brother disappeared with the Reaper, but as to when he fell, and how, I have no clue."

"Well, lucky it is then that you met me, isn't it?"

"It is?"

"Ah, that's the spirit, boy. Question authority, that's my motto, but don't you be questioning me too much now." Neal studies the end of his beard and shakes his head at the damage the fire has done to it. "Damned gremlins," he mumbles. Then with a sigh he turns his attention back to Bran.

"Now listen, you great hunk of meat. I, unlike others I might mention, have learned some." Bran waits expectantly but the little man says no more. Finally in exasperation he leans over Neal and gives him his most intimidating look.

"If you don't tell me what you know, you nasty little man, I shall step on you." Bran regrets his words almost immediately, but Neal doesn't. He breaks up laughing.

"Oh, aye, aye, you are learning. Why, before this is over I might do a great deed for the O'Neals. I may teach the heir how to develop a personality." Then as quick as that, Neal's grin and laughter is gone. He looks at the woods around him then leans toward Bran conspiratorily.

"It is said, lad—not by people, mind you, but by the creatures of the forest—that there is a wizard in these mountains." Neal bites his lip. "A wizard who took no part in the war here five years ago, a wizard so hidden that no others even know his name.

"It is said this wizard is looking for something, some answer, and he collects things. Old things, things not of this world, things like the Reaper."

"And you think this wizard killed Sean and took the Reaper?"

"Hold on, lad; you're jumping to conclusions.

Whether he had anything to do with your brother's death, I can't say. After all, in a war there's lots of ways to get yourself killed, now aren't there?" Bran says nothing, just stares into the fire, his thoughts far away.

"Bran, lad, it's the only lead we have. Even if this wizard doesn't have the sword, I'm thinking he'll most likely have an idea where it is, if anyone does."

"Where can we find him?"

"Well now, that's the hard part, isn't it?" Neal's small hand pats Bran on the knee. "No one, nothing, knows where this wizard is exactly. They know only that he lives in these black mountains somewhere, and they know he makes things."

"Things?"

"Creatures, monsters—have you not wondered why this place is so devoid of life? Have you not met any strange creatures here, like those ugly little brutes we killed?" Bran shakes his head and relates his story so far. The two talk long into the night, making plans. Finally Neal offers to let Bran sleep while he watches through the night.

"You see, unlike you great ox people," Neal says, "the Wee Folk, the only civilized people in this sad land, I might add, rarely need sleep. We really have far too many other things to do to be bothered with such nonsense." Bran foregoes asking just what it is the little people are so busy doing and accepts Neal's offer. For the first time since the council at Loguire's hold, the young warrior sleeps soundly.

The next morning Neal wakes Bran by pouring water over the warrior's head. As Bran wakes, sputtering, the little man turns back to the fire, where a pot boils. Where he found a pot, Bran has no idea. Once again, he decides it's best not to ask.

"Now, you lazy sod," Neal starts, "I want you to drink all this nasty stuff I've cooked up. It'll heal you of all the cuts and bruises you've picked up in all your grand"—Neal stresses the word—"*battles*, you hero you." Bran sips the stuff slowly. It *is* nasty, like drinking mud mixed with salt. But he can feel it working and soon he feels strong and fresh.

"Now, lad, that's all I can do to heal you. You must make sure not to fall all over those big feet of yours any more, 'cause I can't be making that potion again." He takes the pot and disappears into the woods, singing a rather filthy song at the top of his lungs.

Bran gathers up his things and carefully sharpens and oils his weapons. Shortly, Neal returns without the pot.

"Now, boy, we're off. Try not to get in my way, will you?" With that Neal turns and heads toward the mountains.

Shaking his head, Bran follows, nibbling on some old bread he had in his pack. Soon the two come to another clearing. An old road cuts through the clearing, the stones still visible through the grass. There is also a trail that seems to be rather new.

"Well, boy, which way?" Bran stares at the two; they both head off toward the mountains. The road surely leads somewhere, but the trail is new. Which way?

Give Bran 1 D6 of hit points from the effects of Neal's potion.

If Bran follows the trail, turn to section 32.

If Bran follows the road, turn to section 34.

* **24** *

Bran knows he must take the fight to the soldiers or he is a dead man for sure. He waits till the hill has slowed their charge a bit, then rushes to meet the warriors halfway. Tucking into a roll to dodge a sword, Bran comes out of it to slice his long sword across a horse's back legs. The animal falls and several of the warriors can't swerve in time. They are caught in the tangle as the crippled animal thrashes about in agony, crushing its rider beneath its weight.

Bran leaps over the mess and straight into another soldier, knocking the man off his horse. As the two fall together, Bran shifts so his enemy lands beneath him. Even as the wind is knocked out of the soldier, Bran slits the man's throat.

Bran scrambles back to his feet, whirling his sword to block a cut coming straight for him. Before Bran can attack, the soldier drops from his saddle, a small arrow jutting from his neck. Neal is doing his part.

The battlefield is in confusion now, with the downed horse still struggling to get up. The three remaining soldiers try to ride Bran down, but the warrior is too quick for them. Another falls to an elven arrow, and Bran takes down one with a slash that cuts through mail, leather, and stomach.

Now only the leader remains.

"Die!" he shouts, and rides straight for Bran. The man catches another of Neal's arrows on his shield and continues to bear down on Bran. Bran barely deflects the leader's sword stroke, and the horse, well trained, gives him a glancing blow with its front hooves as its rider turns to attack again. Three times the two warriors clash; three times Bran is nearly undone. The fourth time he is ready.

As the soldier comes by again, Bran braces himself. He blocks the sword stroke with his short sword, but his long sword darts past the soldier's shield and impales him through the heart. The soldier crashes to the ground. The horse rears and screams frightened by the loss of its rider, then it runs off, closely followed by the other riderless mounts. Bran just watches them go. He should try to catch one but he is tired, too tired to care.

"Well, lad, that was some fine fighting. And make no mistake about that," Neal says. "But you look battered, lad. Perhaps we better rest in those woods before we continue."

If Bran decides to rest, turn to section 30.

If he decides to continue, turn to section 27.

✻ **25** ✻

Bran approaches the little man carefully. Before he can say anything the creature speaks.

"Well, you needn't be thanking me for my help," he says.

"Thanking you?" Bran's voice is shaking. "Why, I came to your aid!"

"Well, mayhap, you did distract the little buggers some, but well, I'll grant we stand even then." The little man pats the ground next to him. "Now sit down, boy. When you burst out of the trees you cried, 'O'Neal.' Are you an O'Neal then?" Bran sits down by his new companion gingerly, muscles aching from the battle. He stares at the diminutive person next to him and gives a shy smile.

"Yes, yes I am. Bran O'Neal."

"Speak up, boy!" the creature roars. "Good God, you'd think a brute the size of you could at least talk loud enough for a normal person to hear."

Bran doesn't really know what to say so he hides his confusion by cleaning and sheathing his weapons.

"Och, now, those are bonny blades." The little man leans over to inspect them. One diminutive hand reaches out to touch the nearest blade. "Fine, fine." He turns back to the gremlin's head he is roasting on a branch over the fire. "You're probably saying to yourself, now how is it that one of the Wee People can touch iron, eh?"

Actually Bran was wondering why the little man was roasting a gremlin's head.

"Well, it's simple, boy. It's cause I'm special, damn special, and don't ye be forgetting it." He turns to Bran, giving the young warrior a hard look from under his bushy eyebrows. "Special, as all we O'Neals are."

"You're an O'Neal?" Bran starts to laugh. This little creature, not over a foot and a half tall, with his preposterous pot belly, and his white hair and beard all turned up and singed at the ends was claiming to be an O'Neal? Hardly likely, "Ah, cousin, excuse me for not recognizing you sooner."

The little man drops the gremlin's head into the fire and leaps to his feet. Putting his hands on his hips he glares at Bran like an old uncle catching a boy stealing apples, but his stance only made Bran laugh louder. Even though Bran is sitting and the creature standing, Bran towers over the creature.

"O'Neal!" the creature shouted in Bran's face. "I'm an O'Neal. Neal O'Neal as a matter of fact, you lummox."

"Neal O'Neal, huh?" Bran finally stops laughing, but his grin still stretches from ear to ear.

"Neal O'Neal, ya little snot." The little man kicks Bran in the knee. "And where are your manners? Why, in my day, no O'Neal would be so disrespectful to his elders, and his betters." With that the creature sits down with a bump and turns his back to Bran. He ignores the warrior, whistling a tune to himself.

Bran waits a moment. He didn't mean to offend the creature, but an O'Neal? Ah, well, he decides, the little man is only trying to be friendly.

"Mayhap," he says, "you're an O'Neal, and how that came to be you can tell me later. First why don't you tell me how these gremlins got ahold of you and what you were doing here in the first place." But Neal O'Neal ignores Bran, whistling even louder. Bran recognizes the song as an old favorite of sailors, having to do with several friendly lasses at various ports.

"Now Neal O'Neal," he says, "I haven't time for this. I'm on a quest that is vital to all

O'Neals." Bran stresses the name. But still he gets no answer.

"Please."

"Ah," Neal O'Neal turns to face the warrior again, "there, you do have some manners after all, you lout." The little man squints his eyes and looks Bran up and down. "Those gremlins, as you call them, the foul beasties, snuck up on me. That's how they caught me, and there were full twenty, no, fifty when they did. And as a matter of fact, Bran O'Neal, I was about to blast them with me arcane magic when you blundered by."

Bran decides it is best to ignore this last part. Getting anything resembling the truth out of his companion is obviously no easy task.

"And as for what I was doing here, well, I'll tell you, cousin," he smiled up at Bran, "I'm on a quest, too. A quest to find the Reaper."

"What!" Bran shouts.

Turn to section 23.

* **26** *

The monster bends its legs, and with one great leap, attacks Bran. The warrior ducks under the attack, rolling to one side. But he doesn't escape unscathed. One of the claws on the spider's leg cuts him across the face.

Bran gets back on his feet just as the monster pounces again. This time Bran rushes to meet the monster, and his short sword scores a wound under the creature's belly. But once more Bran fails to avoid one of the claws. The two continue their bizarre dance of death for some time, and both are spattered with blood.

Neal stands some twenty feet away from the two combatants. He takes aim and rapidly fires his thin black arrows. Unfortunately the arrows seem to have little effect. Though he has managed to hit the monster several times, it seems unaffected by its wounds.

In desperation Bran changes his attack. Instead of aiming for the body, he focuses on the monster's legs. As the creature leaps again, Bran dodges to one side. His long sword flashes out in an arc and severs the claw from one leg of the monster. At first it seems unaffected by the wound, but when it next tries to attack, it stumbles on its injured leg.

Bran darts in seven more times, each time

©1986

severing a claw. The creature can no longer keep its balance and collapses in a pool of its own blood. It thrusts a large rock at Bran, nearly catching the warrior off guard. Even so, he cannot dodge the missile completely and it catches him in the shoulder. His left arm goes numb and his short sword falls from nerveless fingers and clatters to the ground.

It is Neal who saves the day. One of his arrows catches the creature in its eye. It drops the boulder it was raising against Bran to try to pull the arrow from its eye. Bran knows this is his only chance.

Recklessly he charges straight on. His long sword sweeps across in a glittering arc, severing the creature's left arm and cutting its head off in the same stroke. The violence of the blow makes Bran lose his balance and he falls to his knees, even as his enemy's head falls at his feet.

Bran drags himself clear of the monster's carcass, slipping in the blood and gore that covers the battleground. His wounds are painful, but not debilitating. He groans as he begins to bind the worst of them.

"Well, lad," Neal says cheerfully as if he had just come in from a wonderful picnic, "you're a fine warrior, I'll give you that. But you should take the time to thank the gods that I was here to kill that monster, or you, lad, would have been one very dead hero."

"You killed?" Bran's voice shakes in outrage. "Why you miserable little dwarf, I killed it!"

"Now, boyo"—Neal shakes his head sagely—"we really must begin working on your personality. Not only are you boring, but frankly you have a warped sense of reality." Neal shakes his finger in the warrior's face. "And I'm an elf, you hunk of meat, not a dwarf. You'd do well to remember it."

The two explore the tower but find nothing there. After Bran has rested for a bit, they again take up their quest, arguing continually, till Bran gives up in sheer exhaustion. He has learned one thing on his quest so far: No one can out-talk an elf.

They continue for the rest of the afternoon. The trail leads them deep into the mountains. The only sound accompanying them is that of the wind howling among the rocks, like some unseen banshee. Finally, in the distance, they see some sort of landmark. It looks like a finger pointing at the sky. The two make their way toward it.

Turn to section 39.

* **27** *

"Nay," Bran answers, "my wounds are but slight, and we have little enough time." Neal nods in agreement and the two continue on, leaving the corpse-littered battlefield behind.

"You're a grand warrior, lad, that's the truth," Neal says in grudging admiration, "but a might rash. Without me to save you, you'd be dead."

"What a liar tha'rt. It's been me who saved you."

"Oh, so that's the way of it, is it?" Neal's voice is impossibly large for so small a person. "How quickly they forget. Sure, and isn't it always so with warriors. 'Twas me who killed the dragon, that's what they say. When in truth 'twas forty men or one good elf. Ah, now that's enough, thou lummox. Why, to listen to you talk you'd have us think you some great hero. Peace, can you humans ne'er tell the plain truth?" The two continue to argue happily for some time till Bran gives up in sheer exhaustion. No one could possibly out-talk the elf.

They walk the rest of the afternoon. The road now leads them into the mountains proper and Bran is getting increasingly nervous. The mountains seem worse than the woods. The only sound is the wind howling among the rocks like some unseen banshee. In the distance they can see a strange rock formation ahead. It looks like a finger pointing at the sky. The two make their way toward it.

Turn to section 39.

* **28** *

The soldiers will be on the two in minutes. Bran looks around quickly. There is a grove of trees to the south. They just might make it. Fighting six warriors on horseback while the two of them are on foot seems foolish.

"Let's away, Neal," Bran says, running toward the trees. "We've nought to gain by getting trampled." But before he has finished speaking, the elf is before him, running at a speed to beat a galloping horse.

"Discretion," Neal cries as he runs, "is the better part of valor, me boyo, and no true elf would let himself be trampled by a horse, noisome beasts that they are."

The race is close, but Bran and Neal get to the woods just ahead of the riders. They waste no time looking back. Indeed Bran can barely keep Neal in sight as the elf darts among the undergrowth. The riders are soon lost behind them, but still the two keep moving.

Finally they reach the far side of the copse. The stretch of woods must have been several miles wide; much larger than Bran thought. Safe for the moment, the two stop to catch their breath.

"Look"—Neal points to the crest of a hill a few hundred yards away—"a trail." Bran nods, still struggling to catch his breath. Neal eyes him for a moment, then smiles. "I said we should have taken the other way."

Turn to section 40.

* **29** *

Bran groans in agony. The pain from his wounds is fading his senses. Everything he can hear sounds as if it is at a great distance, while his sight blurs all the world to grey.

It is over. He is dying. He has failed. Failed his quest, his family, his honor. He feels no fear, just despair.

As Rory O'Neal predicted, Bran's failure has dire consequences for his family. Without the Reaper, the retainers of the O'Neals lose heart. Unlike times past, when the Castle O'Neal is besieged, the sappers and miners do not desert. Even the peasants know that the star of the O'Neals has fallen and that there is no point to resistance.

The castle falls to the rebels in less than three

weeks. Sir Rory O'Neal and his wife die defending their home, as do all of their warriors.

The failure of Bran's quest heralds the death of his entire family and seals the fate of the bravest warriors of Gramarye, the O'Neals.

If you wish to try again, start over with Bran in section 1.

✳ **30** ✳

"I think it best we head for the woods and there spend the night," Bran answers. "I'm sore hurt and 'twill do no good to cause my own death through overeagerness."

"There's wisdom there, lad," Neal agrees, "though how you came to find such is beyond my ken. I warrant everyone is bound to do the right thing now and then."

Bran ignores him and the two make their way to the woods. They make camp and Bran spends the rest of the day healing himself as best he can. Perhaps fighting the soldiers wasn't the brightest idea.

Neal spends the night lecturing Bran on how a true O'Neal should act, and trying to teach the young warrior how to tell a good dirty joke. Bran does his best to ignore him. Finally he gets the elf to be still and allow him to get some rest.

"Sure, sure, go to sleep, you brute," mutters

the elf. "Leave it to old Neal O'Neal to watch for the beasties of the night. Worry not, if aught occurs I'll tend to it. After all, you're really only a help to me as a target. You can do that part sleeping as well as awake. No great loss, huh, though O'Neals used to be heroes. Now, now, ye gods, it's enough to try an old man's patience."

The next morning, Neal starts to talk again the minute Bran wakens. Bran puts up with it all through his breakfast. Then the two return to the road and continue on their way.

The road leads them into the mountains proper and the emptiness of the place makes Bran increasingly nervous. It's worse than it was in the woods, for here there is noise, but it is only the sound of the wind whipping through the rocks. The wind's weird howling sound almost seems directed at the two, as if the mountains themselves were outraged that the travelers dare to invade them. Neal pretends not to notice though Bran can see that even the elf is a bit unnerved. After several hours steady walking they see a strange rock formation ahead. It looks like a giant black finger pointing at the sky. Warily the two move toward it.

Bran recovers 1 D6 worth of hit points back due to his resting, along with any hit points he gets back due to any magic he uses.

Turn to section 39.

* **31** *

Bran turns to face the bricked-up doorway of the tower. With a crash it explodes, hurling chunks of brick and mortar all over him and throwing him to the ground.

Still coughing from all the dust, he hears a growl, like that of a dog. Looking up at the now open doorway he sees a horrifying sight. For there, standing not ten feet from him and ready to pounce, is the most frightening monster he has ever seen.

The main body of the creature is that of a giant spider, more than ten feet long. Its body is covered with mottled grey fur and its legs are brown with white dots. But the worst part is what juts up where the spider's head should be. It is the trunk of an ape, its fur matching that of the spider body. But its face is that of a man, a man in horrible pain. The eyes dance about wildly beneath overhanging brows. The mouth is twisted in a grostesque smile; black foam froths from its white lips. Its monkey paws reach for Bran in spastic grasping motions.

Bran leaps to his feet, his blades whirling in front of him, as he prepares to fight to the death.

SPIDER MONSTER
To hit Bran: 14   To be hit: 15   Hit points: 15

Section 32

Damage from paws: 1 D6+2 Damage from swords: 1 D6+2

If Bran wins, turn to section 26.

If he loses, turn to section 91.

Remember Neal's help has already been calculated into the creature's statistics.

* **32** *

Bran considers for a moment. The road is old, and a new trail, well, someone must have made it. Who? Whoever it was, he decides, is probably someone they should talk to.

"The trail," he says and starts walking.

"The trail," Neal mimics. "Well, if something goes wrong, don't blame me. I would have said the road." Bran doesn't bother answering.

The two make good time. Despite his small stature Neal seems able to effortlessly keep up with Bran's long legs. The trail leads toward the mountains in a rather aimless manner, seeming to backtrack on itself for no particular purpose. But bit by bit the two O'Neals get deeper into the mountains.

After an hour they come to a crevasse that bars their way. Posts show them where a bridge had once been anchored. Neal examines them carefully.

"This rope was relatively new, boyo; someone cut it, and not long past, I'll warrant. You'd think visitors weren't welcome in this place." Bran says nothing, looking down into the crevasse. The bottom is lost in the black shadows far beneath him.

"Well," he says, "it's only about twenty feet across."

"Oh, yes," Neal answers. "We can do it with our eyes closed."

Bran looks down at his companion and asks, "Can you do it?"

In answer the elf walks back about ten feet on the trail, then he runs straight at the crevasse. Right at the lip he launches himself in a spectacular leap that clears the gap easily. Bran shakes his head.

"Well, hero, can you do it?" the little man asks. Bran sneers, then he, too, moves back from the edge to give himself some running room. He times his leap well, but it'll be close.

Roll 3 D6.

If the total is less than or equal to Bran's Dexterity value, turn to section 40.

If the total is more than Bran's Dexterity value, turn to section 33.

* **33** *

As Bran nears the midpoint of his leap he realizes he will be just a bit short. He hits the edge of the crevasse with his knees, and before he can catch himself he begins to slide down.

Frantically he grasps for handholds, but he continues to slide down the rough slope. Then he feels a sharp pain in his leg and suddenly his descent stops. Turning carefully he sees he has slammed into a jutting rock and it is all that stands between him and death. Neal's head appears above him.

"Nice leap," he says. "Too bad you don't have any rope."

Rope, Bran thinks, rope. He forgot about his rope. Carefully he reaches into his backpack and withdraws it. He throws one end up to Neal.

"Prithee tie this round something solid!" he shouts.

"Nah, nah, tie it round yourself. I'll pull you up." Bran stares at the diminutive figure, not even trying to hide his doubt. But Neal waits him out, and finally with an oath Bran ties the rope about his chest.

Incredibly, the little man pulls the warrior up, till Bran lies panting on the lip of the crevasse.

"My thanks," he says shakily.

"Your thanks . . ." Neal smiles. "Ah, what a

bonny hero you are. Why didn't you just use the rope to cross the bloody thing?"

"I forgot."

"You forgot." Neal slaps his palm on his head. "Ah, powers preserve me, the lad has no brain, no brain at all."

Subtract 1 D6 from Bran's hit points due to the damage he took in his fall.

Turn to section 40.

* **34** *

"Well," Bran says aloud, "let's continue down the road. Surely it will lead us to people, mayhap to the wizard himself."

"Mayhap to the wizard himself," Neal mimics. "Mayhap so, boyo, but if things go awry, blame thyself. I would have picked the trail."

"Then you should have," Bran answers, leading the way down the road. The two move at a good pace. Somehow, despite his tiny size, Neal keeps up with the warrior effortlessly. The path here is getting steadily steeper and the mountains can now be seen clearly. Bran shudders at the sight of them. They seem full of sharp and bitter peaks, and even the trees on them seem to be black.

As they come to a bend, Neal stops suddenly.

"Riders," he says, grasping Bran's shoulder, "but there is no cover here. How came they so close without a noise?"

There are half a dozen soldiers. They wear livery unfamiliar to Bran. All are well armed and armored, and they are riding toward the O'Neals at a gallop. The leader points directly at Bran and Neal.

"There they are! Get them!" he cries out.

"Ah, we're undone, lad," Neal shouts. "They've seen us, and they want us. It's run or fight now."

If the two decide to fight, turn to section 37.

If the two decide to run, turn to section 28.

∗ **35** ∗

The light from the bizarre lamp hurts Bran's eyes. It has a strange disorienting effect and for a moment he loses his balance. The room is circular, about ten feet in diameter, and bare except for the altar and the things on it.

"Have care, lad," Neal says, but to Bran the elf's voice sounds faint and far away. He moves toward the altar, staring at the sword lying there. There can be no doubt: It is his brother's weapon. He reaches out to grasp it, then pauses in midmotion when he sees a small piece of parchment laying on the far corner of the altar. He picks it up and examines it carefully. It has words written on it in a thick, bold hand:

WHAT IS THE ANSWER TO THE RIDDLE OF THE WORLD?

WHERE IS THE PLACE DEATH'S SWORD WAS MADE?

HOW CAN AN ISLAND MAKE ITS OWN RULES?

WHY DO I EVER HEAR THE CRY, "O'NEAL, O'NEAL, O'NEAL . . ."?

Bran stares at the words trying desperately to understand them. Death's sword is obviously meant to signify the Reaper, but what does the question about the island mean? What is the riddle of the world? He shakes his head in confusion. Whatever this bit of doggerel is about, it surely has some connection to his quest, else why would the last line be concerned with the cry of the O'Neals? Who is the writer? How did his brother's sword come here? Is Sean still alive? The questions seem uncountable.

It is only as he thinks that, that Bran's eyes turn to the ceiling to wonder at a new oddity. The ceiling of the room is round also, but it is covered with little glass globes; all look to be filled with some sort of green smoke that drifts hazily in the containers. This is too much, he thinks, turning back to the entrance to ask for Neal's advice.

But the entrance is dark. Bran can see nothing beyond it. But then he realizes that there is more to it than that. The entrance is closing, closing like a wound healing, closing with him inside!

Quickly Bran reaches down and grabs the sword from the altar. Even as his hand touches it the globes begin to fall from the ceiling. They break open as they land, releasing the strange smoke that they held.

"Trap!" he shouts aloud and dives toward the gap while smoke slowly fills the room as hundreds upon hundreds of the glass globes splinter about him.

Roll against Bran's Intelligence value to see if he holds his breath and doesn't inhale the poison gas.

If the total is greater than Bran's Intelligence value, subtract 2 D6 from his hit points immediately. If that brings him to 0 turn to section 93. If not, turn to section 41.

If the total is less than or equal to Bran's Intelligence value, roll 3 D6 against his Dexterity to see if he escapes from the cave in time.

If the total is less than or equal to Bran's Dexterity value, turn to section 41.

If the total is greater, turn to section 94.

* **36** *

"Hold, boy," Neal whispers in his ear, "can't you see there's no floor in there and that something is moving below?"

With Neal's help Bran lowers himself onto what is left of the support structure for the floor of the tower room. It is pitch black below and he can't see anything. But he can hear something breathing down at the bottom of the tower, something big, something moving closer.

"Ye gods!" Neal's voice shrieks from the darkness. "'Tis some sort of spider devil." The elf shouts out a word, and Bran is blinded momentarily as the elf summons light from the inside walls of the tower. And now, in that light, he can see what Neal was shouting about.

The drop is a good twenty feet beneath the warrior and somehow, ten feet under Bran's position, Neal is standing on an old beam facing a nightmare from Hell. The main body is that of a spider, ten feet long. It is covered with mottled grey fur and its legs are brown. But the worst part is what juts up from where the spider's head should be. It is the trunk of an ape. Its hair matches that of the spider body, but its face is that of a man, a man in horrible pain. The eyes dance about wildly beneath overhanging brows. The mouth is twisted in a terrible, grotesque smile, and foam froths from his white lips. The creature's monkey paws reach toward Neal with spastic grasping motions. Bran has no time. The creature will soon have the elf in its grasp, and somehow Bran knows the creature possesses terrible strength. With a great cry he leaps down onto the monster and the two fall to the floor of the tower.

The creature lets out a high-pitched howl as Bran's short sword stabs its body. With one convulsive movement it throws him from its back. Then it smashes into the bricked-up door of the tower. Even as Bran follows, he sees that the seemingly blocked opening was designed to break easily when struck from within. The creature was not trapped in here by someone. It was stationed here, and the doorway was a trap. Anyone who alerted the creature to their presence would have had a shock as the monster smashed out through the fake wall.

His whirling blades flashing before him, Bran leaps after the foul creature to dispatch it.

SPIDER MONSTER
To hit Bran: 14   To be hit: 15   Hit points: 15 Damage with paws: 1 D6 +2 Damage with swords: 1 D6 +2

Subtract 1 D6 from the monster's hit points; that is the damage it takes when Bran leaped on it. Remember, Neal's help has already been calculated into the creature's statistics.

If Bran wins, turn to section 26.

If he loses, turn to section 91.

* **37** *

The soldiers will be upon them in minutes. Bran looks around. There is a copse of trees to the south, but he doubts they can get there in time. Otherwise, there is nowhere to hide. He draws his swords. Six horsemen, well, there's nothing to be done about it.

"We fight," he says.

"Och, grand. I was afraid you were going to say something like that," Neal answers.

Bran moves off the road to stand atop a tiny hill. At least the rocky ground beside the road will slow the riders and Neal stands with him.

The riders urge their steeds on, and without a battle cry, indeed without noise except that of the horses' hooves, the soldiers charge the two.

SOLDIERS
*To hit Bran: 14   To be hit: 13   Hit points: 5
Damage with sword: 1 D6−1   Neal's damage with swords: 1 D6+2*

Neal's help in the battle is already calculated in the odds.

Section 38

If Bran wins the fight, turn to section 24.

If he loses, turn to section 29.

* **38** *

The tower is some thirty feet high. It is made of dressed stone, but the stone is strangely wet, as if it were sweating. Bran's feet continually slip as he climbs.

Bran pulls himself up hand over hand, but it is slow work. The rope absorbs the moisture from the stone and is getting more and more slippery. Suddenly, Bran's hand closes on a particularly wet spot. Before he can shift his grip he begins to slide. He can't stop himself, but he continues to hold on to slow his fall. He hits the ground hard, but no real damage seems to have been done. As he stumbles to his feet he hears a strange rumbling coming from the tower.

"What?" he cries, as he struggles to draw his weapons.

Bran takes 1 D6 hit points damage from the fall.

Turn to section 31.

* **39** *

They approach the strange object at sunset. Several roads and trails join at this point. One road is paved in strange, black rock. Bran and Neal give little thought to paving stones as the towering stone marker holds their attention.

It is a marker, but what it was meant to mark neither can guess. It is twenty feet tall and is made of the same black rock as the road. It is shaped like a finger, but the hand it is modeled from must surely have come from Hell.

On close examination the first thing Bran notices is the nail of the finger—actually it's more like a claw—which gleams with an unhealthy green tint in the fading light. From where Bran is standing it looks as if the claw has been honed to a sword's sharpness. The skin of the finger seems leprous, covered with scabs and open wounds that seem to run with diseases. Bran shudders at the sight of it.

"By all the powers," Neal mutters, "what sort of mind would shape such a twisted image?"

"I misdoubt me," Bran responds, "but that ere our quest is through, we'll discover it."

The two separate to seek what clues the marker may hide. Bran wonders what rock this marker is made of. It seems almost alive, and whenever he turns away for a moment, it seems that some of the sores on the hand disappear while new ones appear. He dares not touch the statue.

"Bran," Neal cries out, "make haste." Bran moves quickly to join the elf. Neal stands pointing at the statue. For once he is silent. Bran turns to see what has caused such unprecedented behavior and is shocked to see an opening in the side of the statue.

It is like a great wound in the finger. Within, he can see a small stone altar. A lamp fashioned from a human skull burns upon it. The light from the lamp is a peculiar shade of yellow that does not so much shine from the skull as bleed from it. A sword also rests on the altar: a sword with an emblem embossed on its handle.

"The crest of the O'Neals," the elf says, but he needn't have bothered. Bran recognizes the weapon. It is the short sword his brother carried.

"Sean!" he cries and leaps into the strange room.

Turn to section 35.

Turn to section 35.

* 40 *

"Well, 'twas not so cruel an obstacle was it?" Neal asks, already turning to walk down the trail.

"Nay, Neal," Bran answers sarcastically, "not cruel at all." Indeed, Bran has given the matter little thought. At present he is more concerned with wondering what would come to pass should he try to step on the annoying little elf. There is still no sight or sound of life on the road and the silence is making them both increasingly nervous. Suddenly Neal signals Bran to halt.

"Ahead, lad." He points straight ahead to a particularly large hill. "What do you see?"

Bran stares at the hill, following the trail with his eyes, as it winds its way, snakelike, to the top. "There, you lummox," Neal hisses, "the top." Bran squints. Now he sees it: ruins of an old tower and a bit of wall.

"Think you anyone dwells there?" he asks.

"Well, if so, they have a fine view of the approaches to their home." Quickly the two move away from the path and approach the hill under the cover of the scrub brush and large rocks that cloak the hillside. Slowly they make their way to the top.

As they get closer to the tower Bran can see that it is in better condition than he first thought. It is round and has only one window that he can see, and that is set high in the wall. No light comes from it.

Finally the two reach a point scant yards from the tower. They note a place where there was a doorway until someone bricked up the opening.

"I think we should enter," says Bran.

"Aye," Neal agrees, "but what cause could there have been to brick up the doorway?"

"Mayhap to keep folk without," Bran responds.

Section 41

"Or to keep something within," Neal adds, handing Bran the rope. "Whichever the case, that window seems the only way in, and I do think we should find out what this place signifies. You'd best be cautious, lad. I'll keep watch." Bran takes the rope and favors the elf with a grimace.

The battlements at the top of the tower look strong enough to hold his weight so he digs into his backpack and brings out two iron bars to lash together into a grappling hook. Bran gets the hook caught over the battlements on his first attempt. Checking his weapons once, he begins to climb.

Roll 3 D6.

If the total is less than or equal to Bran's Dexterity value, turn to section 2.

If the total is greater than Bran's Dexterity value, turn to section 38.

∗ 41 ∗

Bran dives through the opening, smashing into Neal who has been standing just outside. The two collapse together in a heap.

"Gods preserve me," Neal cries, "I'm squashed."

Bran rolls off him, gasping for fresh air.

Neal goes up to the boy to slap him on the back (which helps matters not at all). Then once Bran begins to breathe normally, the little elf sits down facing him.

"Lad, lad," he says, his voice quite serious, "that was a damned fool thing to do."

Bran just nods, though he has no idea what the elf is talking about. He is still too light-headed to think straight.

"You jumped in there like a shark snapping up a fish." Neal bites his lip. "I tried to warn you, but you were in before I could do more than begin." Neal tugs at his beard. "Bran, I tried, I tried to follow you, but something held me back. I called to you, but—"

"I heard naught."

"What?"

"I couldn't hear you, couldn't see you from in there." Bran's hand strays across his brother's sword. Then he hands Neal the scrap of parchment he found. "We were expected, Neal. 'Twas a trap."

The elf ignores the paper and grasps Bran's knee saying, "I . . . I worried for you, lad. Without you, this quest can't succeed."

Bran smiles briefly in response, but his thoughts are elsewhere, considering the import of finding his brother's sword. He knows what it must mean. If someone had his brother's lesser weapon, then the same person must even now have the Reaper.

"The Reaper," he murmurs to himself.

"We've much to consider, lad. Things are taking a very nasty turn, make no mistake of that." Neal tugs Bran's arm. "Come on, lad, we'll find a place to camp, a place to plan."

Wearily Bran follows the elf, his mind echoing with one question: Is Sean dead?

Neal leads Bran to a small overhang that's sheltered on two sides. They don't dare to make a fire and Bran is exhausted; the gas from the globes still makes his limbs feel incredibly heavy. Though he wants only to sleep, Neal keeps him awake long enough to tell exactly what happened to the warrior within the strange statue.

"This is bad," Neal says as Bran finishes the story, "bad. Whoever designed that place is a magician of great skill."

Bran has no answer to that; he is too tired. He curls up and in moments is asleep. His last sight is of the little elf, sitting cross-legged, his outline framed by the stars. Sean's sword lies across his knees and Neal is staring at the parchment in his hand as if he can read it in the dark. He probably can, Bran thinks, and with that thought he falls fast asleep.

The next morning he wakes feeling a bit stronger, but the quest is exacting its toll. How long can he hope to keep up this pace, let alone survive? The only good that the day has brought is that he has shaken off the effects of the strange smoke.

"Bran," Neal says as the warrior begins to prepare his miserable breakfast, "I've thought long about all this."

"Indeed?"

"Aye." The elf passes Bran his brother's sword. "It must be the wizard who set the trap and for some reason the O'Neals are very important to him."

"You think he had something to do with Sean's . . . disappearance?"

"Oh, Certes, he had everything to do with that." Bran looks up. "In fact," Neal continues, "I'm sure that he has the Reaper."

"Indeed?"

"Assuredly," the elf replies. "That must be what he means by death's sword, but why he would want to know where the sword was made I have no idea."

"Because," Bran says between bites, "it's made of a metal unknown on Gramarye."

"What?"

"The Reaper—no one knows where it came from. The first O'Neal brought it here from some faraway place. It is made of a metal lighter and stronger than any other known, and the blade never dulls."

"What is the answer to the riddle of the world?" Neal quotes. "Of course. It makes sense."

"What makes sense?"

"All of it. Your brother's fall, the theft of the

Reaper, even this bit of lousy poetry. Oh, aye, it adds up right enough."

"Not to me."

"Well, that's to be expected," Neal answers, but he grins at the face Bran makes. "Well, lad, it's not your fault, I guess, that you were born human, I mean. We all have our burdens to bear."

The warrior makes no answer, prefering to wait the elf out. He knows if Neal has ferreted out some secret, he won't be able to keep it to himself.

Add the short sword to your list. Every even battle round Bran fights, add +1 to the damage he gives.

Turn to section 46.

* **42** *

One of the creatures facing Bran rears its bearlike head and howls, while shaking its double-bladed ax at the young warrior. The monster is over seven feet tall and wears chainmail armor. Its companion seems a bizarre mixture of monkey and frog. It wields a two-handed sword with apparent proficiency. The two rush to intercept Bran's charge.

The three meet with a crash. Bran uses his long sword to parry the ax, and his short sword to counter the monkey-frog's blow, then Bran continues his forward movement, tucks into a roll, and dives between his two antagonists.

In an instant, Bran is behind the two and his long sword slices out to cut a deep gash on the bear-thing's thigh. Unfortunately, the other monster is almost as fast as Bran, and his sword misses the young warrior by only a hair-breadth.

Bran realizes that he must defeat the monkey-frog first. It is the real danger here. He feints at the bear-creature with his long sword, forcing it to stumble back. Then Bran parries the great two-handed sword with his short sword. While his opponents recover, Bran dodges inside the monkey-frog's guard. Smashing his shoulder into the creature's chest, Bran hooks his right leg behind his enemy's foot. The monster crashes to the ground and before it can recover Bran's sword severs its neck. Then Bran whirls to face the remaining creature, but this time he isn't fast enough. The ax crashes into his chest, severing mail and muscle, and Bran falls to the ground bleeding and unconscious.

He wakes to see Neal standing over him. Bran feels a weight on his chest. Standing there is the pixie, Sting. The little creature smiles.

"He healed," it says in its high-pitched voice.

"You healed me?" Bran asks.

"Yes, now help." It leaps off of his chest. Bran sits up. He is sore, but that is all. He examines his chest. The chainmail is ripped there but other-

wise there is no sign of his wound, a wound he would have sworn was mortal.

"Hurry," Sting shouts, "hurry, help lady, dungeon, help."

"We *will* help, Sting, just lead the way," Bran answers. The creature runs down the hallway and Bran and Neal chase after it.

The pixie leads the companions to a room off the corridor. The room is a study of some sort. The walls are covered with wood paneling. Sting rushes to the far wall and touches a baseboard. There is a click and a doorway is revealed.

Sting gestures for the other two to enter, then it changes back to wasp form. A strange blue glow comes from its insect body that sheds enough light for Bran to see by.

The secret door opens into a narrow passage which is part of a maze of hidden corridors. Finally they come to a circular stairs which goes down.

Sting flies unhesitatingly down the stairs and the companions quickly follow. At the bottom is a small square room. Sting buzzes over to one wall, which, for no apparent reason, opens up silently. The pixie-wasp flies through the doorway.

Bran and Neal exchange one quick glance. Then they too dive through, ready for whatever lies beyond.

Sting has healed Bran. Bring Bran's hit points to the value prior to this fight. Bran's chainmail has been ruined. He no longer gets any bonus for wearing it.

Turn to section 51.

∗ **43** ∗

Well, it's obvious in this land he can trust no one, so Bran chooses the safe path. But he knows to choose his words carefully. It wouldn't do to antagonize the giant when, after all, he might be telling the truth.

"Thank you for your offer, Fergus MacCallean," he says aloud, "but we must decline. Neal and I have no time to spare. We must find the wizard as soon as possible, though we wish you good luck in your endeavors." For a moment the giant says nothing. Finally he shakes his shaggy head as if in agreement.

"I understand, lad." He picks up his ax. "I shouldn't trust me either, were I in your place. The wizard's keep lies due east. In the end all paths from these mountains lead you there." He gives them one more fierce grin. "Good luck in your quest, Bran O'Neal. Perhaps we shall meet again." And with that the giant walks away, his strange feet making no noise as he goes.

"Well, that's that," Neal says. "And surely this is turning out to be a remarkably strange day." Bran says nothing, watching the giant dwindle in the distance. Now he regrets his decision. There was a nobility to the giant such as Bran had never encountered before. With no more discussion, the two companions head east, each keeping his thoughts to himself.

Several hours later the two stop to eat. The land is crushingly empty. The sparse vegetation is grey and bent. It is as if something is drawing the life from the whole land.

"Listen," Neal whispers.

Bran concentrates and finally, under the howling of the wind, he hears the unmistakable sounds of battle. These last hours he has been steadily regretting his choice not to join MacCallean, and the prospect of action is more than he can resist. He is already running toward the noise before he thinks to shout to Neal. "Anyone fighting in this wasteland needs help."

But Neal is already racing ahead of Bran. Obviously he, too, is looking forward to the prospect of a good brawl.

They run for ten minutes before they can see the battle. On a hilltop a group of men have locked shields. Scrabbling about them are some twenty creatures. They look like the gremlins that attacked Neal, but these are larger, standing some five feet tall.

"What are those?" Neal skids to a stop, staring at the monsters.

"Who knows," Bran answers, "but the men wear the colors of MacCallean."

"Then we know who to fight," Neal shouts,

running again toward the fight. Bran draws his weapons and follows, part of him is wondering— do they really know who to fight?

GIANT GREMLINS
To hit Bran: 14   To be Hit: 11   Hit points: 4
Damage with spear or club: 1 D6−2
Damage with sword: 1 D6+2

Ten of the gremlins detach themselves from the main group and charge Bran and Neal.

If Bran wins, turn to section 58.

If he loses, turn to section 95.

* **44** *

It is a hard choice for Bran, but he decides that the attack on the wall doesn't really need him. After all, two of the captains will be leading the attack there and the men will follow them more readily than they would an upstart knight. Besides, Fergus will need all the help he can get if he is to save his wife.

"I will go with you, Fergus MacCallean," he says. The giant rewards his decision with one of his sharp-toothed smiles. Bran and Neal follow the army to a position directly in front of the main gates. Together the three wait for the battle to begin.

Bran is caught off guard when he hears the cry of O'Neal coming from Fergus's men as they storm the north wall. He smiles to himself, his heart filled with pride at the sound of his clan's name.

"You've done well," Neal whispers to him. "You've done the family proud, Bran." Bran does not answer, watching the great gate of the castle as if he could pull it open with his will alone.

Suddenly the gate crashes to the ground, and the warriors about Bran rise up out of the morning mist like heroes from an ancient epic. Fergus leads the charge, his great voice bellowing over and over.

"O'Neal! O'Neal! O'Neal!"

Bran takes up the cry and, with Neal scampering at his side, runs at full speed toward the open gate. The enemy within tries to hold the way, but there are only a handful of guardsmen and they are overwhelmed by Fergus and his warriors.

Bran reaches the main courtyard without finding anyone to fight, then a strange lizardlike creature rears up out of the dust to bite at him with a fang-filled mouth. Bran's long sword catches the creature through the neck even as two of Fergus's men hack the monster's body. That enemy defeated, the warriors advance in an irreversible flood of vengeance.

Turn to section 63.

* **45** *

Bran waits for the monster to attack. The creature approaches the young knight warily. It swings its weapon back and forth in some strange rhythm whose purpose is known only to it. Then with a roar it swings the weapon down. Bran catches the blow on his two crossed swords, but the power behind the swing forces him to his knees.

Bran is barely able to dodge the next swing, which smashes into the ground inches from the warrior. Such is the strength of the monster that the very castle seems to shake when its weapon hits the parapet. Bran's short sword snakes out to score against the monster's calf, and the creature leaps back with a bellow of pain.

Bran regains his feet and presses the attack. His swords leap out again and again to draw blood from the creature. Bran dares not slow his attack for a moment. He cannot allow the monster time to attack. The monster's club is a terrible defensive weapon, but Bran knows that if it connects even once he is a dead man.

Step by step Bran forces the giant back. But Bran is getting tired. He knows that if he doesn't finish the creature quickly, he is done for. With a yell Bran leaps in the air, swinging his long sword downward at the doghead. The creature's club intercepts the blow. The sword sticks fast into the wood of the club. As Bran's feet touch the ground he leaps again, this time straight at the monster.

Bran's short sword leaps out and drives straight through the creature's furry chest, splitting the heart beneath. Bran collapses upon the corpse, too exhausted to stand or to care if an enemy stabs at his now-exposed back.

"Well done, lad." Neal's voice is husky. The elf helps Bran turn his vanquished enemy over. Bran sees that Neal is covered with bites and scratches, but he looks basically sound.

Neal looks Bran up and down.

"Ah, lad, you're sorely hurt," he says. For the first time Bran can feel the burn of the wounds he has taken from the dogman. Sometime during the fight the monster had bitten his arm, and there is a deep gash on his side.

"Neal," he says, "I fear I can help no more in this battle."

"Not so," says a high voice. Bran looks up to see Sting standing there.

"You have fought well, warrior," Sting says, "and I will do what I can to heal you, that you may fight still better."

Sting heals Bran 1 D6 hit points.

Turn to section 52.

* **46** *

Bran doesn't have to wait long. Neal watches the warrior clean his weapons. Finally he sighs loudly.

"Well, aren't you going to ask me what I've discovered?" he asks.

"No." Bran refuses to even meet the little man's gaze.

"Well, belike I'll tell you anyway." Neal sits down in front of Bran, waiting until finally the warrior turns to face him. The elf nods in satisfaction, sure that he has the other's attention now.

"Gramarye is an island," he declares.

"Everyone knows that."

"To be sure, but did you know that there are other continents?"

"Yes."

"Aye, but did you know that those other continents have not only different weather—much hotter—but also different trees and vegetation, now?"

"Uh, well, I've ne'er given it a thought."

"Well, it's obvious our warlock friend has." Neal crosses his arms and smiles with satisfaction.

"That's it?" Bran shakes his head. "That is your great discovery?"

"That's not all I've found," Neal answers. Bran waits for him to continue, but the elf just stares at him with a self-satisfied smile.

"All right, all right, what else?"

"Well, 'tis obvious, is it not?"

"Nay, 'tis not."

"Well, then. 'What is the answer to the riddle of the world?'" he quotes. "In other words, why is Gramarye so different from the rest of the world? 'Where is the place death's sword was made?' We know that is about the Reaper. Where does it come from if not Gramarye? 'How can an island make its own rules?' Once more, why is the weather here different, the very vegetation? And last but not least, 'Why do I ever hear the cry, "O'Neal, O'Neal, O'Neal"?' Your family is different from the other powers on Gramarye. There's the sword, the chainmail you wear, your strange fighting system that's been handed down in secret through all these years, there's your treatment of the peasants, and your treatment of witches."

"I still don't see."

"'Tis easy, boyo. The original O'Neal must have come from somewhere other than Gramarye. That explains the sword, the mail, and the different attitudes toward ruling your family has always had."

"And this wizard, for some reason, wishes to discover from whence we came?"

"Aye, and for several reasons. One, there is the new knowledge to be gained, and knowledge is

power. Two, the sword and mail. Now if someone had the formula to make such metal, why,
they could be rich, or build nigh invincible
armor. And the third reason—the reason I think
first captured the wizard's interest in all this—if
the weather and vegetation is different here,
there must be a reason. Someone or something is
responsible for it, and if our nemesis can discover what or who that is why, to be sure, he'd be the
most powerful man alive."

Bran does not answer, trying to take it all in.
There was a vastness to this, a danger far beyond
his own imaginings. The one thing that is clear to
him is that this wizard is dangerous, very dangerous. He thinks about the creatures he has met
and fought thus far on his quest. He knows that
they are the creations of their unknown enemy,
and one who can—who would—make such
monstrosities is sick, a twisted and dangerous
person who must be stopped.

And there is one more thing, probably what is
of most concern to Bran. Whoever this wizard is,
whatever his goal, Bran is now certain that he is
the major force behind Sean's disappearance,
and even if he'd done naught else, for that the
warlock would pay.

"We must find this wizard and stop him."

"Oh, aye, lad, that we must, for I fear this
wizard plans nothing less than the domination of
all of Gramarye."

"Of that you need have no doubt," an unknown voice answers. Bran and Neal leap to

their feet to face the strangest of all the strange creatures they have so far met.

Turn to section 49.

* **47** *

Bran decides it is best he stay on the wall. The fighting is fierce and every sword is needed. Even as he makes his decision he hears Neal cry out. Turning, Bran sees two of the elite guards go down to a single blow of a huge dog-human's mattock. The creature is nearly the size of Fergus. Its face is that of a dog and its body is covered with short brown fur. It has human feet though, and human hands, and its blood-shot eyes are full of a dark intelligence. By its side is a four-foot-tall gremlin. With a yell, Neal throws himself upon the gremlin. There is no one else near enough to help, and Bran knows that he must defeat the giant dog creature alone.

DOGMAN
*To hit Bran: 10   To be hit: 13   Hit points: 16
Damage with sword: 1 D6+1   Damage with swords: 2 D6*

If Bran wins, turn to section 45.

If Bran loses, turn to section 55.

* **48** *

Bran falls to his knees, the agony of the wizard's fireballs finally reaches him. He feels rather than sees Fergus and the others stir from their ensorcellement. Soon he is surrounded by people and voices congratulating him, but Bran can make nothing of it. All he wants now is to sleep. He can celebrate later.

He wakes to find Neal's familiar face smiling at him. Bran struggles up on an elbow. He is in a room in the castle, lying on an incredibly soft bed covered with rich furs and silks. His wounds have been carefully bandaged. Bran sighs with contentment.

"Ah, so you're finally up, you lazy ox."

"Glad to see you, too," Bran answers. Neal's grin grows even larger.

"Oh, lad, you've done the family proud, that you have."

"The lady? Fergus?" Bran asks.

"They're both fine, and happy as two peas in a pod." Neal leaps off the bed. "The castle is ours, lad, and all of the wizard's dogs lie dead, too. And you, my boy, are the hero of the day."

"I don't feel much like a hero."

"Och, of course you do." Neal points to a chest. "Now, you'll find some clothes in there, me boyo. Fergus and the lady are waiting to greet you. We've much to discuss." Neal walks out at that. Bran gets up, surprised at how well he feels. He opens the chest to find rich clothing within, and is pleased to find them a surprisingly good fit. Just as he finishes dressing, a young soldier enters to escort him to Fergus and Margaret. Bran is a little embarrassed by the open admiration in the young man's eyes.

Fergus and Margaret sit at the end of a small hall on matching wooden thrones. Neal and Sting stand next to them. Bran is surprised to see that Fergus's eldest daughter, Maeve, is waiting with the others. For once the girl looks happy. There's no one else in the room.

"Bran O'Neal, knight of the realm," Fergus bellows out, looking rather silly in finery much too small for him and a chair that can barely hold his weight, "there are no words for what I and my family owe you. Ask what you will of us and we will do all in our power to grant your wishes." Bran is silent for a moment. Then he speaks, for once his voice steady and strong.

"Assist me against the black wizard," he says. "Aid my quest to recover what is mine."

Fergus nods. Surprisingly, it is Margaret who speaks. "Bran O'Neal"—her voice is gentle, though the marks of her imprisonment cannot be totally hidden—"we will do all that we can to help you in your quest. Of that you may be sure."

"Give me an army that I may storm the wizard's hold."

"That we cannot do, lad," Fergus answers sadly. "Our losses were great in taking the castle and the wizard has at least a thousand at his command. I couldn't hope to muster such a force, for months yet at least."

Bran thinks for a moment. Time is of the essence. Even now his family's castle could lie under siege. He knows what he must do, but he is afraid. Such a thought would have surprised him short weeks ago, but he has learned much since that time. Only a fool is unafraid. The brave are those who face their fear and conquer it.

"I must go to the wizard's lair. I must confront him and defeat him myself," Bran says. He knows the statement is as much for his own sake as for the benefit of the others. Neal gives him an encouraging wink. Indeed Neal looks to be bursting from his pride in the warrior.

"Yes," Fergus says, "that is your destiny, I fear. For whatever reason it is you, the O'Neal, that must meet the wizard and cast him down."

"We can help in this," Margaret adds.

"I would go myself," the giant's eyes flash, "but, alas, I cannot. All who served the wizard have a compulsion. We may fight his warriors, but we can raise no hand against him. In such a quest I would be more hindrance than help." Bran does not show his disappointment at this. The giant's strength would have been a welcome aid.

"It is as you say, Fergus MacCallean," Bran says. "It is my destiny and I alone must face it."

"Ah, not quite alone, boyo," Neal interjects.

"We can offer no warriors for your quest," Margaret says, "but we can give you these." She nods to Maeve who shyly approaches Bran with a strange, thick glove and a small vial.

"The vial holds a potion," she says to him. "If you swallow it, it will give your body a strange power to repel metal weapons. It can only be used once and the effect does not last long. It can save your life." She looks up at Bran and he is shocked by the beauty of her eyes. "Brave knight," she whispers.

"The glove is enchanted, too," Margaret continues. Bran barely hears her. He is filled with a strange feeling of happiness by simply staring at Maeve. "Put it on, Bran." Bran does as she says. It is like a gauntlet but thicker; the inside is some strange black substance, the outside leather. On the back is a small red gem.

"When you touch the ruby stone," Fergus continues, "while holding a metal weapon, it will fill that weapon with lightning, making its bite much more powerful."

"It is the greatest treasure of the MacCalleans," Margaret says. "We were able to hide it from Balar, but we give it freely to you."

Bran flexes his hand in the gauntlet carefully. This is a mighty weapon, one worthy of a king. "I cannot accept such a talisman," he says.

"You can," Neal chirps in.

"You must," Margaret adds. She looks at her daughter who is still gazing at the young knight with adoring eyes.

Even in his exuberance over the gifts Bran is only too aware that Maeve is standing just a few feet away from him.

She smiles. "Perhaps," Margaret says, "it will

one day return to this family." But Bran does not understand her meaning, though Neal catches it, and is hard-pressed not to give way to laughter.

"Two more things we can give you," Fergus says. "One is knowledge of ways to enter the wizard's lair, and the second is soldiers."

"But you said—" Bran starts.

"You misunderstand," Fergus continues. "True, we cannot storm the wizard's castle, but when you return, you will need help to protect your clan's lands. This we will give you, to begin to make up for the evil we have done, by standing firm in this civil war beside Catharine, our Queen."

The next days are truly the happiest of Bran's life. He is healed of all his hurts and he practices daily with the magnificent gauntlet. Scouts have been sent out to track the wizard, and the castle is repaired and cleansed of its war wounds. But best of all is Maeve.

In between the feasting in Bran's honor, the war councils, and training, Bran and Maeve spend what time they can together. The whole castle watches their budding love with glee, but the two are unaware that others have noticed their feelings. Bran begins to realize that should he succeed in his quest there is one more thing that he might ask of Fergus MacCallean.

The golden days pass quickly and finally all of the scouts have returned. The wizard's hold is only a day's march away. It is a large place tucked away in a valley, surrounded on all sides by mountains. A great wall protects an area of several square miles. In the center the wizard's castle stands atop a large hill. The area for miles around is heavily defended, both with outposts and monsters. Getting to the castle will be at least as hard as getting into it. Finally the wisest approaches are narrowed to three.

"The mines," Fergus tells the young warrior, "lead straight into the castle, but the way is dark and unsure, and no doubt guarded. The stream" —he points at the map—"leads to the far side of the south wall, and underneath to wrap around the hill the castle stands on. The south wall is the least defended of all the walls, but where the water passes through is a thick iron gate, one that will be nearly impossible to get by. The third way is the most perilous, the direct road to the castle. It is traveled by the wizard's men. But on the other hand it is the last place he will expect to see you. I doubt that you could sneak by the guards, but if you get close enough you may be able to get over the wall."

Bran has been healed of all wounds. Add the gauntlet to his list of items. When Bran uses the gauntlet in battle add +3 to the damage his opponents take when he hits with his long sword. He can use this 8 rounds; after that the energy in the gauntlet is drained. Add the vial to Bran's list. He may use it once in battle. If the enemy is using metal weapons, subtract 2 from their chance to hit Bran. The potion may only be used once.

If Bran goes by way of the mine, turn to section 61.

Section 49

If Bran follows the stream, turn to section 65.

If Bran takes the road, turn to section 74.

* **49** *

Standing before them is a giant. The creature stands some nine feet tall. He is well muscled and wears a humongous mail shirt that hangs to his knees. He holds a large, double-bladed ax in two scarred hands. His face is human, with grey hard eyes and a thick black beard which matches the mane of hair on his head, but his legs are fur-covered and end in clawed toes. Perhaps most unsettling of all is the long monkeylike tail that waves in the air behind him.

Bran readies his weapons but makes no move to attack. In spite of the many horrors he has faced, there is such an aura of power emanating from the giant that he hesitates. But not Neal.

"And who are you?" The elf looks like a mouse challenging an alley cat.

"I, little man," comes the booming answer, "am Fergus MacCallean, lord of Castle O'Clare." The giant makes no move to threaten them.

"No, you are not," Bran shouts back. "Fergus MacCallean was slain five years ago when the King burned Castle O'Clare. The MacCalleans were one of the leaders of that black rebellion."

"I am Fergus MacCallean, the very one you speak of."

"Fergus MacCallean was a man," Bran answers, "not a, a—"

"A monster?" the giant finishes, but still he makes no threat of violence.

"Sure now," Neal interrupts, "if you're Fergus MacCallean, then how is it that you're not dead and not a man?"

"That is the story I have come to tell you."

"Oh, you have, have you? And tell me, are you, along with being a hairy giant, a bard as well?"

"That I'm not"—the giant's voice is tinged with exasperation—"but I will tell you that story, and you will listen." His voice echoes among the rocks as he shouts the last words.

Bran and Neal exchange glances. What have they got to lose? Neither wishes to antagonize the giant without cause. So, saying nothing, they move away from the giant and sit on the ground. Bran does not sheathe his weapons.

The giant smiles broadly at this, showing his rather sharp teeth. He lays down his ax and sits across from the two.

Looking up at the giant Bran feels small for the first time in his life. This, he thinks, must be how he looks to Neal.

"I'll make the story short and simple, as simple as I can," the giant says. "I *am* the same Fergus who rebelled against the King, and Castle O'Clare was taken by His Majesty's forces. And I was dead, or near enough to it—who could tell

©1986

the difference?" The giant's grey eyes turn away from them, but Bran catches a glimpse of something in them, something remarkably like fear.

"I was 'rescued,'" the giant nearly spits out the word, "by the man who was been behind the civil war all along."

"This man," Neal interjects, "wouldn't happen to be a wizard, would he?"

"Oh, he's a wizard all right," the giant answers, "and his heart is as black as Satan's own." The giant grabs a ten-pound rock. The companions watch in silence as the huge hand closes slowly, crushing the rock between his thick fingers. "And he has power," he continues, "power to do many things. Power to take a man and make him into a monster."

"Are you saying that this wizard made you into, uh, a giant?"

"That he did, while claiming to save my life by the process." The giant looks sadly at the broken rock in his hand. "Such a life. I gained strength, but I have lost everything else: my honor, my family, and the woman I loved most in the world. I lost it all for that madman and in return he made me into a freak."

Bran and Neal are both shocked by the intolerable grief in the giant's voice. They look at each other, but what answer is there to such a horrible tale?

"Fergus MacCallean," Bran says quietly, not quite daring to look at the giant's face, "whatever reasons led you to rebel against your righteous liege lord, whatever wrongs you may have done in such a war, assuredly you have paid for your actions." It was the best he had to offer to comfort the giant.

"As one knight to another, Bran O'Neal, I thank you for those words."

"How do you know his name?" Neal shouts.

"Why, my spies told me."

"Spies?" Neal leaps to his feet. "What are you telling me? Who can spy on Neal O'Neal without his knowledge?"

"He did sneak up on us without us hearing him," Bran says.

"Nah, nah, spying indeed. Art thou then not in league with this black-hearted wizard, our sworn enemy? Art thou not his servant then by your own admission?"

"I was," the giant answers, his voice low. "I was. But after he made me into . . . into what I am, I escaped his black castle. I went back to my lands, gathered others to my cause, and for these last five years I have made war upon his forces."

Bran and Neal say nothing. The giant's words ring true, but still they are not fully convinced. No word of such a war has reached beyond these mountains.

"Come to my camp. I could use two with your skills." The giant stands. "Tonight, I again make war against the dark one. I and my men will attack Castle O'Clare where the wizard's right hand has taken residence." He looks down at the two. "Join me," he says. "If, as you say, the wizard is your enemy too, then together we can strike a hard blow against him, whilst I revenge myself for the fall of the MacCalleans."

Neal turns to Bran, leaving the decision up to him. Bran is unsure. The giant seems sincere and such an ally would be a great help. Also his chivalry is stirred by the thought of the wronged lord fighting to regain his castle lost through war and treachery. On the other hand, Fergus admits that he had aided the wizard who started the civil war against the King; the same war his brother disappeared in, and that he had somehow been spying on Bran and Neal. What should they do?

If Bran decides to go with Fergus, turn to section 57.

If Bran decides not to join the giant, turn to section 43.

* 50 *

Bran wastes no time trying to guess how Balar set the arrow on fire. Charging the wizard, the young warrior cries his clan's war cry. "O'Neal!"

For a moment Balar seems to hesitate. And in a flash of inspiration Bran knows why: The wizard fears the O'Neals. But the mage quickly recovers. He points his finger at Bran, crying out some arcane word. Bran feels something slam against his chest, throwing him off his feet. Instead of resisting the magic, Bran uses the motion to do a back flip, and twists to land back on his feet like a cat. He charges again.

Balar pulls a black ball out of some hidden pocket. The ball levitates above the mage's head and Balar cries another arcane word. This time the effect is quite different. The ball bursts into flames and shoots straight at Bran. The warrior is unable to dodge the fireball completely and he is forced to roll to put out his cloak which is on fire.

But in his singlemindedness Balar has forgotten Neal and the elf fires three of his arrows, one right after another. Again the wizard uses his magic to render the bolts useless, but in the intervening time Bran regains his feet and is able to move within sword range.

Bran's long sword comes down in a sweeping arc aimed at the wizard's neck. But in midstroke some force intervenes and stops the sword's movement. At the same time the wizard casts another spell. This time a dazzling kaleidoscope of light bursts in the air between the two antagonists, and the light blinds Bran momentarily. The wizard begins to laugh.

His laugh is out short when Bran's short sword slices through his chest. Long is the training the heirs of the O'Neals must go through in order to gain their fighting skills, and many are the times that such practices are held in the pitch darkness.

Still, the wizard refuses to die, and Bran is struck again with a blow from an unseen force. This time it is his head that takes the blow and the warrior falls to his knees. But Bran does not release his hold on the short sword. He pushes the weapon deeper into the wizard's vitals. At the same time he drops his long sword, and with his free hand catches the mage behind the knee and flips him onto his back.

In desperation, Balar creates another fireball, but his concentration is broken when Bran slams an elbow into his stomach. Before the mage can recover, Bran regains his long sword and sweeps the mage's head off with a single blow.

"That," he says, "is for Sean."

Roll 1 D6 to determine the extent of Bran's injuries.

If this brings Bran's total to 0, turn to Section 29.

Deduct any hit points Bran has lost and turn to section 48.

* **51** *

The scene Bran and Neal burst in to is a picture from Hell and both step back as they take it in.

The room they find themselves in is a torture chamber. It is large, thirty by fifty feet. The roof is lost in the shadows. At ten-foot intervals along the walls torches burn fitfully in the dank air. Skeletons, some with pieces of flesh still on them, hang in chains along the far wall. In the middle of the room is a rack. A fire pit at the foot of the horrid instrument outlines it in a lurid glare.

Section 51

An abnormally tall human stands next to the rack. He is dressed in a black robe. At his feet is a woman, her face pale, blood streaming in her eyes from a cut upon her brow. The man lifts her up by her hair. He is facing away from Bran and Neal, all his attention centered on the doorway to the room.

There Fergus MacCallean stands motionless with several of his warriors. They are surrounded by a strange, green dancing nimbus. Each of the warriors' faces is contorted into a soundless scream. Their weapons lay useless at their feet. Even as Bran and Neal watch, one of the warriors falls to the ground, blood rolling from his nose, ears, and mouth. The sight of this wakes Bran from his shock.

"O'Neal!" he cries, charging the man in the robe who he knows must be the wizard Balar. Sting flies at his side and Neal's bow twangs as he fires an arrow at the wizard's black heart.

The wizard turns to meet this new threat. The cowl falls from his head baring his face. His features are perfect, his hair long, curling and black, his eyes a beautiful green. But for all his physical attractiveness there is something inhuman about the wizard. He sneers at the companions, disdaining to feel threatened by their attack. Neal's arrow burst into flames while yet five feet away, falling harmlessly at his feet. Balar shoves the woman away and crosses his arms, intoning some magic words that Bran knows are meant to presage his death.

But Bran feels no fear. Here is evil, true evil.
He knows it in his heart, and he will defeat this
evil. He will destroy it.

WIZARD BALAR
To hit: 12   To be hit: 14   Hit points: 12
*Damage with fireball: 1 D6 +2   Damage with
sword: 1 D6*

*Balar uses a combination of magics to fight. The
fireballs are his offensive weapon.*

If Bran wins, turn to section 50.

If he loses, turn to section 82.

* **52** *

Sting heals Bran as the witch woman had so long
ago. He feels much better, though still sore.
Nonetheless he is once again ready for action. He
props himself up on his elbow and looks about.
The dog monster's corpse lies beside him, its
still-hot blood steaming in the morning air. The
catwalks are full of bodies, both human and
otherwise, corpses twisted at odd angles. The
carnage is terrible, unlike anything the young
warrior has ever imagined. But there is no fighting going on around them at present. Apparently
Fergus's men have captured the wall and moved
on.

Section 52

"Where?" Bran says, but he is unsure how to finish his sentence.

"To dungeon," said Sting. Bran looks at the tiny man.

"Dungeon?"

"Dungeon," the pixie says, "secret way, hurry, lady in trouble, hurry." With that he turns into a wasp again. Bran gives Neal a weary look but Neal just shrugs, as if to say, "He's a pixie, not an elf."

The wasp buzzes around the two again till they get to their feet. Then they have to run to keep up with the creature. It leads them swiftly to the tower. The two have to leap over the bodies that litter the room, and they nearly fall the length of the stone stairs to keep the strange creature leading them within sight. The wasp stops at the bottom of the stairs, staring at the far wall. For no discernible reason a secret door opens.

The creature buzzes around the two again, then goes through the doorway. The companions follow, their weapons ready. The doorway leads into a small, narrow passage that works its way gradually downward. The walls are wet and the footing treacherous. It is dark but a strange witch glow that appears around the wasp gives off enough light for Bran to watch his footing.

The passageway continues for some time, then ends in another black wall. The pixie changes into a man again.

"Through here," he says, "dungeon, lady

needs help, hurry." With that he touches the wall which opens outward. Bran and Neal leap through.

Turn to section 51.

* **53** *

That night Bran and Neal join the captains and Fergus to plan the raid. A soldier brings them to a large hall where the giant and his four captains are sitting around a large oak table. Quickly Fergus fills them in on the plans.

It seems that the castle is held by one of the wizard's protégés, a warlock of some skill called Balar. The walls of the main keep have been repaired recently and are in good shape. Within are some two hundred of the wizard's army. They are creatures that are neither monsters nor men, but bizarre mixtures of both.

"Each of the warriors waiting within has been twisted by the wizard's magic," Fergus says, "even as I have."

Fergus has some five hundred men to take the castle. They are all seasoned veterans. Also, Fergus has created an elite corps of warriors, all of whom had once served the wizard, and all, like Fergus, have been part of the wizard's demonic experiments. There are twenty-five of them and they are ferocious fighters.

Section 53

"You have the manpower," Neal says, "but it will take a long siege to take a castle as well fortified as you say this one is."

"Well, as for that"—Fergus smiles, baring his sharp fangs—"I have a secret weapon, the same secret weapon that spied on you unknowingly." Fergus claps his hands. There is a buzzing sound and Bran and Neal are surprised to see a wasp land on the table. The wasp is at least four inches long. For a second the creature wavers, then standing there is not a wasp, but a tiny man no larger than Bran's hand.

"Well, by the gods," Neal says, "someone smaller than me." All the warriors at the table break up at that. Fergus explains that the little man (a pixie, not an elf, Neal is quick to point out) will fly into the castle. As the main part of the army assails the walls, Sting, the pixie, will cut the rope holding the main gate closed. A second force will then rush in, overthrowing the guards at the gate and make straight for the dungeon to free Lady Margaret.

"Speed is the main factor," one of the captains says. "We must burst through before they have a chance to organize themselves."

"Margaret," Fergus adds, "thanks to Sting, knows our plans. We've sent a knife to her, so even if we cannot get to her quickly she should be safe." The others nod at that, and Bran is pleased to see not only the determination on the others' faces but their obvious professionalism.

The rest of Bran's night is spent poring over maps of the castle, which all the warriors of Fergus's army have memorized. The plan is to leave three hours before dawn and strike an hour before sun up. That way the guards on the night shift will be tired, and their relief will not be awake yet.

Bran doesn't even bother to sleep in the few hours left after the meeting breaks up. He is too excited. This will be his first real battle, and the fact that the war cry of the O'Neals will signal the attack has him counting the minutes till it is time to leave.

Finally the time comes and the army quietly says good-bye to its loved ones and moves off into the night. The march to the castle takes an hour, but to Bran it seems like three, and he can barely restrain himself as he waits for the signal. Fergus comes up to where Bran and Neal are.

"Well, Bran O'Neal," the giant whispers, "will you be going with me to attack the gate, or will you lead the attack on the wall?" Bran is silent for a minute. If he goes with Fergus he will have a better chance to help the giant free his wife, but if he storms the walls he can lead his first attack. And he knows that the fiercest of the fighting will be at the wall.

If Bran is down hit points, he receives 1 D6 due to the camp healers.

Section 54

If Bran decides to storm the wall, turn to section 87.

If he decides to join Fergus at the gate, turn to section 44.

* **54** *

Bran decides it does not matter whether or not Neal knows a way. Fergus is going to need all the help he can get, and from the sounds of fighting he can hear ahead, the sooner he can help Fergus the better.

"Follow MacCallean," he says. Neal just nods in agreement, and the two race down the hallway.

After a hundred yards the hallway branches into other corridors. The bodies of five of the defenders of the castle lie in one branch, a sure sign that this is the direction the giant has taken.

This corridor is littered with bodies, both human and otherwise. There are doors spaced every ten feet or so. Some have been broken open, others left alone. The whole area echoes with the clash of arms, but Bran is unsure which way the giant has gone.

"Where?" he says. As if in answer there is a crash ahead of him and one of the doors splinters outward. Suddenly facing the two companions are three of the wizard's strange warriors, one holding a huge ax and the other two wielding swords.

"That way," Neal shouts. He leaps into the air to crash into one of the warriors wielding a sword. It is an incredible feat considering the creatures are a full twenty feet away. Bran shouts inarticulately and races to help the elf.

Neal and the soldier he attacked roll about on the ground in a desperate battle. The other two creatures face Bran, battle lust burning in their red eyes.

MONSTER GUARDS
To hit Bran: 13   To be hit: 12   Hit points: 8
Damage with ax: 1 D6
Damage with sword: 1 D6+2
Damage with swords (Bran's): 2 D6

There are two of the monsters and Bran must fight both of them.

If Bran wins the battle, turn to section 59.

If Bran loses the battle, turn to section 42.

* **55** *

Bran waits for the monster to attack. The creature approaches warily. It swings its weapon back and forth, back and forth, in some strange rhythm known only to it. Then it swings the weapon down with a roar. Bran catches the blow on his crossed swords, but the power behind the swing forces him to his knees.

Bran is barely able to dodge the next swing, which smashes into the ground only inches from the warrior. Such is the monster's strength that the very castle seems to shake when the weapon hits the parapet. Bran's short sword snakes out to score against the monster's calf, and the creature leaps back with a bellow of pain.

Bran regains his feet and presses the attack. His swords leap out to draw blood from the creature again and again. Bran dares not ease his attack for a moment. The monster's club may be a poor defensive weapon, but Bran knows that if it connects with him even once he is a dead man.

Bran forces the giant back step by step. But he is tired. He knows if he doesn't finish the creature quickly, he is done for. With a yell Bran leaps in the air, swinging at the dog-head with his long sword. The creature's club intercepts the blow. The sword sticks fast into the wood. As Bran's feet touch the ground he leaps again, this time straight at the monster.

His short sword leaps out to drive straight through the creature's furry chest. But as Bran's weapon seeks the monster's heart it howls once and bites the warrior's shoulder deeply. The pain is unbelievable. Now Bran rolls away from the monster. He looks up to see the creature trying to rise, but Neal leaps onto its chest and drives the short sword deeper into its breast. With that the monster dies.

"You'll not die this day," Bran hears Sting say. But he blacks out and hears no more.

Sting heals Bran. Bring Bran's hit points up to half his original.

Turn to section 52.

* **56** *

"By the powers, what a smelly brute," Neal says, kicking the corpse of the monster he fought. The creature looks like nothing so much as a giant ferret.

"Neal," Bran says, "thank God you're safe."

"Hah," Neal snorts, "'tis me who needs to worry about you. Why, when you are even half the warrior I am, then you can waste time worrying about me."

"What now?" Bran asks.

"What indeed," Neal says. "I suppose we search for the dungeon."

"Dungeon," says a squeaky voice, "dungeon, help lady, hurry."

Running down the hallway toward the two is the owner of the voice, none other than the pixie, Sting, himself.

Section 56

"Hurry," Sting screeches, "hurry," and he races past the two.

Bran looks at Neal. The elf just shrugs. Bran smiles and then takes off after the pixie with Neal right behind him.

The pixie leads the companions to a room off of the corridor. The room is a study with walls covered with wood paneling. Sting runs to the far wall and touches a baseboard. There is a click and a doorway is revealed.

Sting gestures for the other two to enter, then changes back into a wasp. A strange blue glow comes from its insect body. It sheds enough light for Bran to see by.

The secret door leads into a narrow passage. Neal and Bran follow the wasp-pixie through a maze of hidden corridors till finally they come to a circular stairs leading down.

Sting plunges down the stairs and the companions quickly follow. At the bottom they find themselves in a small, square room. Sting buzzes over to one wall which, for no apparent reason, opens up silently. The pixie-wasp flies through.

Bran and Neal are quick to follow. The knight's swords glitter in the strange glow of the pixie light and Neal brandishes his deadly bow. They are ready for whatever may await them.

Turn to section 51.

* **57** *

The two companions follow the giant, trying gamely to keep up with his tremendous pace. For all his bulk Fergus moves quickly and lightly, his strange feet making no noise as he moves nimbly among the rocks.

He is following no discernible track, at least none that Bran can see. But he doesn't fear treachery. Something tells him that Fergus MacCallean, giant though he is, is a trustworthy and honorable man.

After little more than an hour the group comes to a halt. In front of them is a tall cliff. Before either Bran or Neal can say anything the giant begins to rap on the cliff face in a long and complicated pattern. Moments later, a door in the cliff face opens up with a terrible grinding noise. Fergus waves the two in.

Bran is surprised by what he sees, for on the other side of the door is not the passage he expected, but a valley, a beautiful valley at least a mile wide and two long. The walls on all sides of the valley are sheer and rise to incredible heights. Here, protected from the wind and whatever demonic influences affect these mountains, the vegetation grows abundantly. Bran can see at least three streams meandering through the valley, and a waterfall pours down not thirty feet from the opening.

Two human guards bow low to Fergus. He salutes the two and continues into the valley. Behind them the door through the cliff closes with a boom.

"It's beautiful," Bran says.

"The valley of Eden," Fergus says, showing another fierce smile. "That's how we call it, anyway. I suppose it might offend some of the good fathers a bit, but nonetheless it seems proper." Bran can see a number of troops in the valley, marching and exercising. In the south corner a small town has been built of stones. Surely, he thinks, hundreds must live here.

"So this is your base, is it?" Neal says.

"Yes, this valley has been a secret of my family for years, since my great-great-grandfather found it when he was out hunting one day," Fergus replies. "Here, all those who lost their homes in the old wars and those who count themselves enemies of the dark one can find refuge and help us to strike back against their enemy."

Two women come running up to meet the companions. One is a girl, no more than twelve years old, who leaps at the giant with a squeal. Laughing, Fergus lifts the girl over his head and swings her about. The other is no more than seventeen, a dark-eyed girl who, if she didn't look so solemn, would surely rival all the beauties in the kingdom.

"These," Fergus says with obvious pride, "are my daughters, Katherine and Maeve. These, my lassies, are two heroes who have come to help us retake O'Clare Castle." Bran blushes to be called a hero, but Neal acts as if he is used to such a title.

"The girls will help you get settled. I must meet with my captains. Afterwards we shall talk." With that the giant marches away. Bran and Neal follow the girls toward the small town. Katherine, the little one, is giddy with excitement and chatters on and on about every little thing, much to Neal's obvious pleasure, but Maeve says nothing, walking ahead, silent.

The girls leave Bran and Neal at a small stone hut. There the two relax. Bran uses the time to clean his weapons and armor. Later, Maeve comes back with dinner for them. Without saying anything, she places the food on the rickety wooden table which dominates the center of the room. Then with a tense good-bye she leaves.

"She sure doesn't like us," Bran says.

"No, it is not you, Bran O'Neal," a voice says. Fergus walks into the room. Inside a building, he looks even more massive than ever. "It is me she doesn't like," he finishes.

"You?" Neal asks.

"Yes, because, because of her mother." Both Bran and Neal wait silently for the giant to continue. With a sigh Fergus sits cross-legged on the rush-covered floor.

"Her mother, Margaret, is a strong-willed woman," he says with a faint smile. "Ah, that she always was." The giant looks away from the other two. "There was a great love between the two of us, at first. But I guess, I guess time and responsibility get in the way. By the time of the rebellion we were barely speaking to one another, for I was so under the sway of the dark one, and Margaret never trusted him, never.

"To make a long story short, it is not just the castle I want back. It is Margaret."

"Margaret," Neal says.

"Yes, the wizard has her imprisoned there, in the dungeon." The giant's hands flex as if he is envisioning a neck to be strangled between them. "He took her hostage to keep me loyal, but still I turned on him." Fergus looks the two straight in the eyes, and again Bran is shocked to see the agony in that gaze.

"Now, Katherine, she knows none of this. I've told her that her mother is safe and staying with her own clan, but Maeve . . . Maeve . . ." but he says no more.

"So," Neal says, "Maeve knows that your war might very well get her mother killed?" The giant has no answer to that. "And so," the elf continues, "she hates you for what she sees as your betrayal of her mother."

"It is not a betrayal!" the giant shouts. "It is what Margaret would want of me. She would despise me if I did not fight." Bran reaches out and grasps the giant's massive forearm.

"Fergus MacCallean," he says, his voice very solemn, "listen well. We shall free your wife and regain your castle. And"—Bran's voice shook with his outrage—"when that is done I shall personally spit this devil wizard on my sword and present his head to you on a platter." Fergus does not meet Bran's gaze. For a moment he is silent.

"I believe you, Bran O'Neal, and I would beg one more favor of you."

"Anything."

"Let my warriors use the battle cry of the O'Neals in our attack." Bran is shocked by the request; it is a thing unheard of. In essence it should mean that Fergus has recognized Bran as his liege lord. Though it is improper to grant the use otherwise, Bran finds he cannot refuse such a noble request.

"You will honor me and my clan for a thousand years, Fergus MacCallean." The giant says nothing more and, with a bow to the two, departs.

"That is as sad a story as ever I have heard," Bran says. But Neal is not listening.

"'Why do I ever hear the cry, "O'Neal, O'Neal, O'Neal"?'" he quotes.

Turn to section 53.

* **58** *

Bran and Neal wait for the giant gremlins to attack. Neal brings down one with an arrow in its eye, and then the true battle begins. In the confusion of the melee Bran loses sight of Neal as he fights for his life.

The monsters are armed with clubs mostly. Two have spears, but they seem inexperienced in their use. Bran's swords flash, and the second of the gremlins falls, its stomach opened by the dancing weapons. In quick succession two more are downed; one of Neal's arrows catches another of the monsters. The remaining five pull back for a moment. In less than a minute's combat half their number have fallen.

Bran takes advantage of the creatures' hesitation and leaps among them before they can organize themselves. His long sword takes off the head of one, even as his short sword plunges deep into the chest of another.

That's enough for the remaining creatures. They drop their weapons and flee. Neal catches one more in the back of its neck with his deadly arrows.

The two companions grin at one another for a moment, then without a word they head toward the hills where the men have routed the other gremlins.

To their surprise they see, outlined against the

sky, the giant form of Fergus MacCallean.

The giant lets out a bellow to welcome the two and waves them up the hill where he is tending two of his wounded men.

"Well met," he says. "It looks like I have you to thank for saving my men."

"Sure, and it was nothing," Neal replies.

"Nonetheless, I am in your debt."

"Think nothing of it, Fergus MacCallean," Bran says. He nods his head to the gremlin bodies scattered about. "If these are your enemy, then we are your friends." Fergus's solemn eyes grow bright.

"Then you'll join us in our attack?" he asks.

"That we will," Neal answers. He puts his tiny hand in the giant's massive palm in a parody of a handshake. "And glad we are that we can be of service to you."

Note any hit points Bran has lost.

If this brings Bran's total to 0, turn to Section 29.

Turn to section 57.

* **59** *

One of the creatures facing Bran raises its bear-like head and howls, shaking its double-bladed ax at the warrior. The monster is over seven feet tall and wears chainmail armor. Its companion is a bizarre mixture of monkey and frog, but it

Section 59

handles the two-handed sword it wields with obvious proficiency. The two rush to intercept Bran's attack.

As they meet with a clash, Bran uses his long sword to parry the great being's ax, and his short sword to meet the monkey-frog's weapon. The knight continues his forward movement, tucks into a roll, and dives between his two antagonists.

In an instant Bran is behind his two opponents and his long sword slices out to cut a deep gash on the bear-thing's thigh. But the other monster is fast and he barely manages to avoid its attack.

After that Bran knows he must defeat the monkey-frog first for it is the real danger here. He feints with his long sword at the bear creature, forcing it to stumble back. Then he parries the great two-handed sword with his short sword and he steps inside the monkey-frog's guard. Bran slams his shoulder into the creature's chest and hooks his right leg behind his enemy's foot. The monster crashes to the ground and before he can recover, Bran's sword stabs through its neck.

Bran whirls in time to meet the other warrior's attack. His sword a whirlwind of death, he savagely counterattacks. In moments it is all over, with his long sword buried deep in the monster's chest.

Breathing heavily, Bran wipes the sweat from his brow. "Neal," he says, "are you unharmed?"

Turn to section 56.

* **60** *

Bran assumes that Neal knows what he is talking about, and he is determined to get to the dungeons before Balar can kill Lady Margaret. Without a word he turns to the door Neal has pointed out and breaks it open with a leaping kick.

He finds himself in a small hallway with a door at the other end. None of the enemy are here.

"Quickly!" Neal yells. Running past Bran, the elf runs straight at the door, shouting some strange words. A burst of light shoots from his hand and hits the door square in the middle. The door rocks on its hinges, then falls straight backward. Bran shouts some incoherent words of encouragement and follows his friend through the now open door.

Both skid to an abrupt stop as they pass the broken door. The room is obviously a bedroom, though no one has stayed here for a long time. The bed and furnishings are covered with dust.

"Somewhere in here," Neal pants, "is a secret door to the dungeons."

Just then, a panel opens up on the far wall and stepping through it is none other than the pixie, Sting.

"Hurry," he cries, waving the two toward him, "this way. Dungeon, lady, needs help." With that he turns and runs back into the darkness. Bran gives Neal a questioning look, and the elf answers with a shrug.

"A Pixie," he said, "by the saints, following a pixie in the midst of a battle. Ah, it's enough to turn my hair grey." Bran smiles and the two rush to the secret door.

Behind the door is a small passageway. The doorway is so low that Bran has to duck in order to enter. The pixie has turned into a wasp again and in that form he gives off a strange blue light, which is barely enough for the knight to see by. He moves as quickly as the tight fit will allow.

In minutes they come to stairs. The wasp plunges straight down them. They are circular and time-worn. Heedless of the danger Bran runs down them at full speed. At the foot of them is a small stone room. The pixie-wasp hovers at one of the walls, and silently a door opens into darkness beyond.

Bran jumps through the opening, his weapons ready. Neal tumbles through, his deadly bow at the ready.

Turn to section 51.

* **61** *

Bran decides to try the mines, even though they will be guarded. Taking the road seems simply foolhardy and following the stream is no good if he has to climb the wall, for he doubts that he could manage the feat undetected.

When Bran and Neal start off the next morning, they are well supplied and both are feeling anxious to see the end of their quest. Scouts from Fergus's clan lead the two for the first part of the journey.

The mountains are still as quiet as ever and Bran feels a strange sense of dread growing with each mile. The rocks here have all been scoured by some fierce wind. The stones are torn and twisted into demented forms. Nothing seems to grow here at all, and even the few streams the small party finds on their way are foul.

Finally, near sunset, the guides stop.

"There." The leader points to a mountain a half mile away. "That is your destination. Do you see the tall stone standing alone?" Bran nods. "Go to that stone and wait for sunrise. The stone has a small hole in its center. When the sun strikes this hole at sunrise it will shine on the mountain's face. Go to that point and press it hard and a secret doorway will open. We do not know for certain whether it is guarded, but my lord Fergus doubts it. Good luck." And with that the scouts leave.

"Sure and they're no end of fun," Neal mumbles, watching the scouts' retreating backs.

"They simply want to get as far away as possible from this mountain before night," Bran says. He looks once at the mountain's darkening face. "I cannot really blame them," he adds.

Section 61

The two pass the night in quiet conversation, going over and over the little information they have on what lies before them. Neither sleeps well and they are glad when the night finally comes to an end.

Quickly they make their way to the rock the scout showed them. As they reach it they see that not only is there a hole in the middle, but the rock itself is carved crudely in the shape of a dying warrior; the howl of the wind is his death scream. When the light from the rising sun hits the sculpture, the belly of the warrior turns red as if blood runs down his stone limbs. The light passes through the hole and hits the mountainside, and Neal rushes to push on the spot before the sun can move. There is a loud crack as an opening about three feet wide by three feet high appears in the mountainside.

Neal bows toward Bran. "Since when this is over," he says, "you will no doubt and unjustly be given all the credit, I'm thinking it is you who should be walking through this nasty little hole first."

Bran shrugs and enters. It is pitch black in the small space. Bran moves onward, trusting to his sense of touch. The tiny passage has obviously not been used in a long while and Bran is hard-pressed to restrain his urge to cough from the dust he and Neal kick up.

After a few minutes of stumbling about blindly —with Neal cursing behind him—Bran tumbles

out of the passage onto a hard stone floor. He listens carefully but there is no sound except for Neal.

"Oh, this is a lovely place," the elf says.

"I can't see anything," Bran answers.

"Meat," adds a third voice.

"Grand," Neal responds, looking around. A bright light fills the room and Bran is momentarily blinded by the glare. When he can open his eyes again he sees that the light is not as bright as he had first thought. It comes from a single torch; a torch held by a creature that looks like nothing so much as a very large rat.

"Meat," the rat-thing says again.

"Wonderful," Neal answers bitingly, readying his bow. Bran draws his swords.

"Fight," the rat says, leaping at them. The creature carries no weapons other than the torch, but his paw-hands are well equipped with five-inch claws.

"What else," says Neal.

GIANT RAT-THING
*To hit Bran: 15   To be hit: 10   Hit points: 30
Damage with claws: 1 D6−2 Damage with swords: 2 D6*

If Bran wins the fight, turn to section 85.

If Bran loses the fight, turn to section 96.

* **62** *

The creatures bear down on Bran but he keeps all his attention fixed on the large net. It floats in his vision like a black wave. He must time the blow perfectly. NOW!

His sword flashes in the sun. It cleaves straight through the net at just the perfect angle. He doesn't sever the net completely, just cuts enough to allow him to leap over what remains. Even as he leaps he realizes that the net was made of metal. He tangles his sword in the damaged net, allowing the creatures to drag him along for a few feet. Then he activates the gauntlet.

Sparks fly from his sword point up to the net and from there to the monsters. They both cry out, dropping the net. Bran prepares for their next attack but it doesn't come. They run away.

The third creature follows them, having failed to capture Neal.

Bran turns to the elf. "They're running away?" His voice wavers in disbelief.

"How not?" Neal answers. "They have many friends nearby."

Bran watches the retreating figures. "This was not a wise choice," he finally says.

"Mayhap," Neal answers. "What have thee heard concerning discretion, and its place in relation to valor?"

"Run, and live to fight another day?" Bran asks.

"Indeed," Neal says, "that seems a sound notion. Let's run then." And the two leave the road at speed.

The mines are miles away and it would take time they cannot afford to reach them, but the stream is barely an hour's journey away, so they choose that as their alternate approach.

They move at a good pace, soon leaving the road far behind. Finally the stream is before them. The banks are steep, but the water is fairly calm. They grasp onto a floating log and ride the gentle stream toward their destination.

Bran has now used the gauntlet. Record this on your record sheet.

Turn to section 69.

* **63** *

Fergus leads his men straight for the main keep, more warriors pouring through the open gate behind him. Many leap from the now-taken north wall to join the fighting in the courtyard. The attackers spread out in a V formation with

Fergus in the lead. His giant ax cuts a blood-drenched path through to the doorway.

This door falls—to the surprise of the defenders—and like wolves among sheep, Fergus and his men scatter them. Bran and Neal push their way to the front ranks, to fight on beside the giant.

The first room they come to is a large banquet hall and the defenders don't even try to hold it. Several doors lead out of this room, all have been shut by the beleaguered enemy. Fergus divides his forces to attack each of the doors, and the giant himself crashes through one door and cuts down the two half men behind it before they even realize what has happened.

"To the dungeons! To the dungeons!" Fergus cries as he leads the attack down a long hallway. Bran and Neal try to keep up, but they soon lose sight of Fergus in the press of men and fighting about them.

"Bran," Neal cries, pointing at a doorway to his right, "I think the dungeons lie beyond." Bran hesitates for a moment. He can hear the clash of weapons and screams of wounded men all around him, the nightmarish sounds echoing all about the keep. Fergus has disappeared down the hallway. Men are still streaming past. Several attack different doors along the way.

Should he try to follow Fergus, or should he trust Neal's advice? Surely Fergus knows the quickest way, but then again Neal would probably not have spoken if he wasn't sure.

Section 64

If Bran follows Fergus, turn to section 54.

If Bran takes Neal's way, turn to section 60.

* **64** *

Bran leaps from the parapet to join the battle in the courtyard. The wall has already fallen to Fergus's men and they can easily defeat the few remaining defenders. But Bran knows instinctively that Fergus will need help to save his wife.

An enemy tries to bar his path. This creature seems human save for a strange beaklike appendage on its face, but its sword work is no match for a scion of the O'Neals. In moments the creature lies dead at Bran's feet.

"My sword for Fergus MacCallean!" Bran cries, raising the reddened weapon over his head.

Turn to section 63.

* **65** *

Bran decides that the stream is his best choice if he hopes to surprise the wizard. The mines are certain to be guarded, and the road, well, an open approach seems foolish. Only blind luck could get them through that way. And trusting to luck is a good way to get killed.

The two plan to leave the next morning. Bran has no chance to see Maeve that night and he longs to see her just one more time. His adventures have taught him much and he knows there is a good chance he will never again see the woman who has captured his heart.

In the morning Fergus and his wife come to see the two adventurers off. The parting is brief. The sooner they are off the better; the fewer people who know that they've gone the safer. Bran is disappointed that Maeve is not there to say farewell.

As if reading his thoughts, Lady Margaret says, "Maeve asked me to give you this." She hands Bran a long scarf. "A fitting token for a noble knight." Bran bows deeply, breathing in the fragrance Maeve has left on the scarf. Resolved to complete his task and return as soon as may be, Bran says his good-byes and he and Neal set out on their journey.

"Ah, 'tis good to be on the road again, eh, lad?" Neal says as they walk along, but Bran has no answer for him. He holds the scarf in his fist, and his thoughts are far from the adventure ahead.

At midday they stop to rest. A half mile ahead is the road that leads straight to the wizard's stronghold. From here the companions will walk off the road, keeping a good distance from it.

It takes most of the day for the two to reach the stream. It is a wide ribbon of water, more a river than a stream, at least that's what Neal claims. Bran doesn't answer. The water is cold, but not too cold, and it moves swiftly. It should bring them to the wizard's hold before nightfall.

The banks are as full of rotten wood as Fergus told them. Bran finds a suitable log and pushes it out into the stream. He and Neal get in the water and drift down the river holding the log.

Twice when they see figures ahead along the streambank, they hold their breath and hide beneath the log to drift by unseen. The cold is beginning to make the two numb and they are grateful when near nightfall they can pull themselves out of the water.

"Och," Neal mutters, "some heroes we are." He sneezes. "Dying of pneumonia is something anyone can do." Bran is too miserable to answer. The two have an uncheerful dinner and then return to the water.

"How much longer?" Neal asks.

"Not long," Bran says. Painfully he raises one hand from the water to point. Straight ahead is a long, dark line. "The wizard's hold," Bran says.

Neal is silent for a moment. "Bran," he asks, "does this journey please you?"

"What?" Bran chokes, accidentally getting a mouthful of water.

"I was just wondering," Neal murmurs. "I don't want you to be saying I've lost my sense of fun, but," he adds, "I'm definitely not enjoying this."

Turn to section 69.

* 66 *

Bran and Neal enter the room. It is large, sixty feet by thirty. There are metal tables along the walls. On the tables are a bewildering array of objects displayed in glass cases. Bran can see that many are weapons but some are unidentifiable.

More tables are set at the end of the room. These are obviously workbenches for they are covered with the wizard's apparatus; and standing next to them is the wizard himself.

He is a tall man, dark-featured and handsome. His clothes are serviceable hunting leathers, and a short sword is strapped to his left side. There is no one else in the room.

"Well," the wizard says, "I had wondered whether you'd reach me, young Bran. I must say you've been giving my pets quite a hard time."

"This is a wizard?" Neal says, but the others

ignore him. Bran begins to walk toward the man, his blades naked in his hands.

"I did not come to talk, wizard." Bran's voice is harsh.

"No, but I suggest that before you start something you cannot finish, you should listen to me." The wizard makes no move to draw his weapon. He just watches. Bran stops ten paces away.

"Talk?" he says. "You and I have nothing to discuss."

"But we do." The warlock gestures at the tables. "Do you know what is displayed here?"

Bran looks around and shakes his head.

"Here, Bran O'Neal, are a variety of instruments, weapons, works of art. Each of them is special. Do you know why?" Again Bran shakes his head. "They are special, warrior, because they are not from Gramarye."

"Ah, from the moon, I'd guess," Neal shouts. He is still down at the other end of the hall, looking at the various displays.

"I think not," the wizard answers genially, "but some could be. You see, that's the problem. I know not where they come from; no one does." The wizard purses his lips together. "Why have you not asked my name?"

Bran blinks, caught off guard. What is this madman going on about? "What's your name then?" he asks.

"'Tis . . ." the wizard pauses, "Donal O'Neal."

"What!" Neal shouts. "Liar!"

"Nay, I do assure you, we are all related."

"That cannot be," Bran says.

"But it is." Donal leans on the edge of one of the tables. "You see, that's how it all started." Neal moves up and stares into Donal's black eyes.

"You're no O'Neal."

"Certes, I am," Donal says. "'Twas the O'Neal fighting style that showed me the way of it."

"What?" Neal says.

"Bran understands." Donal nods to the warrior. "My great-grandfather was a second son, and a far more worthy heir than his eldest brother. When his brother became the clan chief he left and came to these mountains. His family assumed he died here, which was all to the good, everything considered."

"I don't understand." Neal moves away, shaking his head.

"He taught his son the fighting secrets of the O'Neals," Bran said, beginning to understand.

"Exactly." Donal laughed. "Of course, it was bound to happen eventually. It's a hard world—the two-sword attack is rare enough to give one an excellent advantage." He smiles at Bran again. "So he taught his son the style, which he wasn't supposed to do. And his son taught his son, and on to me. Add to that the fact that the O'Neals have always understood the value of magic and well, here I am."

Bran is silent for a moment. "Let's say you are an O'Neal," he says, "let's say your great-grandfather did break his oath, but that still doesn't explain this." He nods toward the tables.

"But it does," Donal replies. "Indeed, it does." He pushes himself off of the table and moves closer to Bran. "You see, Bran, that was the first clue, a fighting style unknown elsewhere in the world. The O'Neals have always been different in many ways." He turns and walks about as he talks.

"'Twas a simple matter to fit it all together. Add in these things, all not from this land. Well, it becomes clear, doesn't it?" He spins to stare at Bran. "Neal O'Neal was created by our great-great-grandfather. Did you know that, Bran?"

"Created, ha!" Neal's voice comes from somewhere among the tables.

"'Tis true. That's how he came to hold the clan name."

"No O'Neal"—Bran's voice is low—"would do as you have, create monsters, betray retainers, sack and pillage for their own greed."

"Greed." Donal shakes his head. "Ah, Bran, your experience is so limited." He moves back in front of the table. "Not greed, lad, but thirst for knowledge. 'What is the riddle of the world?'"

"Sure, and you know, lout," Neal says.

"No, not yet, but soon." The wizard bites his lip. "I'm missing something. It's obvious that Gramarye is a colony. But whose? I still don't know why the weather and vegetation is different here than on the other continents. How can all this be done? I don't know, but I will find out."

"Whatever your reasons," Bran says, "they do not justify your evil."

"Bran, think, boy," Donal responds. "The weather is controlled, our ancestors created Neal."

"They did not," Neal answers sullenly.

"It is recorded," Donal answers. He turns back to Bran. "Such power, boy, power to reshape the very world."

"As you did those poor creatures you use as your army?" Neal says.

"No!" Donal shouts. "No, they are not creations, but mutations." The wizard's voice goes quiet. "I do not know how to create new life, how to do the things our ancestors did." He turns back to Bran, his eyes feverish. "Bran, we are cousins. You've proved yourself to be extremely adept. You could join me, help me. Between us we can find the answers, the answers to the secret of life itself."

"And when you have those answers?" Neal asks.

"Why, then we rebuild, create a whole new world, a world of magic, of beauty."

"Ah, and you have such a fine eye for beauty that you can choose what's best for all?" Neal snaps.

Bran is silent for a moment, thinking carefully. After a moment he reaches his decision. "No more talk, wizard," he says. "I shall answer your riddles with three of my own." He straightens up, his features fierce.

"First," he says, "if we gain the power, can you be certain that what you would build would be better than what we have? Second, would you share such power? And third, where is the Reaper?"

The wizard goes to a table and picks up a long object. "Here is the Reaper," he says. "Your brother brought it to me."

"He would never betray his honor!" Bran shouts.

"Sean heard rumors of me, five long years ago. He sought me out, as you have. I offered him the chance to join me. He refused me as you have." The wizard sighs.

"Sean," Bran hisses.

"I fear," Donal answers, drawing his short sword, "that your brother did not give me the Reaper willingly."

Bran's reaction is instantaneous. The time for talk is over. "O'Neal!" he cries, attacking the wizard.

WARLOCK
To hit Bran: 10   To be hit: 12   Hit points: 15
Damage with swords: 1 D6   Neal damage with swords: 1 D6+2

Bran's spells will not work as the wizard will negate them. Donal's magic has been calculated into the odds.

If Bran wins the battle, turn to section 68.

If he loses, turn to section 83.

∗ **67** ∗

Small puffs of dust rise up from the floor as Bran and Neal begin to walk along the passageway. "It's been some time, I'll warrant," says Neal, "since the wizard's servants have done any cleaning along here."

Bran chuckles a bit at the thought and turns to smile at Neal in thanks for his attempt to relieve the tension. "'Tis strange," he says, continuing the joke, "I've not noticed such lapses elsewhere along this route." Suddenly Bran stops walking and holds up a hand for Neal to do likewise. It is rather odd that this passage alone shows such signs of neglect. And he's never seen dust quite like this. . . .

"Is something amiss?" asks Neal.

Bran shrugs, shaking off the feeling that something is not quite right. "I'm just tired, Neal. At least I'll warrant that's all it is. It's been a long day, and I'm starting at shadows. Let's go." As he takes his next step, he hears a sharp click.

He has only enough time to shout "Trap," before the noise is followed by a sudden movement in front of them.

Section 68

Roll 3 D6.

If the roll is less than or equal to Bran's Dexterity value, turn to section 77.

If the roll is greater than Bran's Dexterity, turn to section 84.

* **68** *

Bran lunges at Donal, his weapons spinning. Donal meets him with the same form. The four swords whirl and crash. Every attack Bran attempts is parried by the wizard, who is uncommonly strong. But Bran's rage sustains him as the two duel.

Bran hears someone pounding on the door which Neal has closed and now guards. Bran knows it is only a matter of time before the wizard's reinforcements arrive. Then he and Neal are dead men for certain.

Bran uses what little witchcraft he can manage, but the wizard repels it easily. Donal replies with a magic blow to knock Bran's guard aside. But the warrior is not so easily thwarted.

Bran is tiring. Both he and Donal are covered with blood from bites of the flashing blades. But Donal's defense is slowly weakening. Donal may have learned the same fighting skills, but in the history of the O'Neals few have mastered them so well as Bran, and his greater skill is beginning to tell. But skill alone is not enough. He must kill the wizard quickly while he still has the strength. He must kill him now.

Bran lunges again and this time his sword goes straight through the wizard's chest, cleaving the heart.

Donal drops his weapons and grabs Bran's shoulder to try to keep his footing. "What," he gasps, "is the riddle of the world?" With that, his hands slip and he falls to the floor. Bran reaches down to pick up the Reaper.

"Sean," he whispers. Just then Neal reaches his side.

"That door won't hold those monsters for long," he says. "Follow me." He darts off to the far corner of the room, Bran following quickly. There is a small wooden door hidden behind one of the tables. Neal pushes it open.

"While you and your friend were chatting," he says, "I picked the lock." The two rush through, relocking the door behind them.

It takes them what's left of the night to win free of the castle. As soon as the wizard was found dead, his creatures turned on each other, struggling for dominance. The whole valley is a battleground, but by seeking to avoid combat, Neal and Bran slip through easily enough.

A week later, Bran returns to his clan home, Fergus and his army are ranked behind him. The castle is besieged, but with the return of the heir, the Reaper, and a fresh army, the sappers and miners throw their support to the O'Neals. Bran's force routs the remaining rebels besieging the castle.

Days later the news comes to the O'Neals that Catharine's forces have crushed the rebellion. Not only that, but it seems that the Queen is to marry Tuan Loguire and there will be a new King, one who plans, the courier adds, to raise the O'Neal to the rank of Baron.

Now that the war is over Bran sends for Maeve. The O'Neals have a wedding to plan, too.

Bran sits upon his father's chair in the great hall. Maeve will be here in less than two days. With her will come her father to pledge his clan to the O'Neals. Bran's mind spins with the memories of his quest. He has saved his family, and defeated an evil and dangerous enemy of the realm. Soon he will join Fergus in the field and they will return to Donal's castle to destroy the rest of the wizard's disorganized army.

His father and mother are more than proud. He is the hero of the Duchy. The news is good: not only will the crown allow the witches more freedom, but a powerful new warlock has befriended and helped Catharine against the insurrection. Bran is pleased to hear that. Now he and his family can develop their magic abilities more openly.

Yes, he thinks, all has come out well, but still something is missing. Glory lasts only for a moment . . . only a moment. He knows he has grown older and wiser on his quest, but he did not find his brother's bones, and, and . . .

"'What *is* the riddle of the world?'" he asks the empty room.

THE END

* **69** *

The water is getting colder and the two companions more miserable. But they can see the wall of the wizard's hold clearly now and, cheered by the sight of it, they hold on, kicking a little to move the log faster.

After another twenty minutes they reach the wall. The water passes under the wall unimpeded, but a thick grate keeps the log and the warriors from following the same path. The two drag themselves out of the water, the cold air biting at them. The sun is nearly down and beside the wall all is in shadow.

"Well," Bran whispers, "I guess over the wall is the only way for us." Neal looks less than cheery at the thought. The wall is a full twenty feet high, and the two can hear the tramping of guards' feet. It seems hopeless and they both know it.

"There may be another way." Neal speaks so quietly that even Bran can barely hear him. "The bottom of the river is very muddy."

"So?"

"So, mayhap the current has softened the bottom beneath the grate and we two strapping heroes can swim down, dig about where the grate meets the bottom, and find room enough to slip through. It's that or—" Neal points to the well-guarded wall.

Bran nods once and quickly reenters the water. Diving deep he pulls himself along to the grate. It's even better than Neal suggested. There is a gaping hole in the grate less than ten feet down. He comes back up and hurriedly shares this news with Neal.

"I warrant 'tis still the best way," the elf agrees, concern evident in his voice and manner, "but I do wonder what made that hole?"

Bran just shrugs; at present they really have no choice. The two swim down to the hole and are through the grate in moments. They allow the current to carry them half the distance between the outer wall and the wizard's keep. Then they drag themselves across the muddy bank. It is pitch dark now.

The lights of the nearest village are half a mile away. The great outer wall of the stronghold is at least a mile long sweeping in a long semicircle from the mountainside. In the center is the wizard's keep.

"The last leg now," Bran says, preparing to stand.

Neal starts to answer but something catches his eye and he tugs Bran's arm and points back to the river.

A shadow is rising out of the river. It is roughly humanoid, completely silent, and massive. This must be the creature responsible for the convenient hole in the grate. In the faint starlight Bran can see the monster is a strange mixture of fish and man, and though it makes no sound and it moves ponderously on land, he can see that it intends to attack.

Quickly he leaps to his feet, his weapons drawn. He cannot afford a long battle for it might alert the wizard. He must kill the creature quickly.

RIVER CREATURE
*To hit Bran: 14   To be hit: 14   Hit points: 20
Damage with claws: 1 D6+2   Damage with swords: 2 D6*

If Bran uses the gauntlet plus while fighting the creature he adds +5 to the damage he inflicts.

If Bran wins, turn to section 75.

If he loses, turn to section 97.

* **70** *

Bran catches the first guard unawares and the spear goes straight through the creature's neck, killing it instantly. Bran spins to face the creature that held the front of the spear. Howling, it raises a sword and attacks. Bran deflects the sword blow and cuts through the creature's thigh, a deep disabling wound, then he spins again to face the two guardsmen who have dropped Neal. A third guardsman he didn't notice earlier has joined them.

Bran throws the spear which hits one of the guardsman in the shoulder. Even as the creature goes down, Bran feels a sharp pain in his back. He turns in disbelief. The guardsman he crippled stabbed him with its knife! The pain is excruciating and Bran sinks to his knees. Something smashes into his face and he falls onto his back, driving the knife deeper. He stares up into the face of one of the guardsmen. It is scale-covered and horned, a devil out of Hell.

"A valiant effort, man-thing," it says, "but futile." It turns away from Bran and shouts over its shoulder. "Kill the other."

"No!" Bran shouts, but he knows it is too late. So far, he thinks, I've come so far, only to fail now. The creature raises its sword for the killing blow. Bran knows he has failed in his quest, but it was not a total failure. The wizard is doomed now, he knows that. One way or the other Fergus MacCallean will avenge the O'Neals. Even as the sword plunges into Bran's breast he is surprised to realize it is Maeve that he is thinking of. It is the fact that he'll not see her again that he regrets most.

Turn to section 29.

* **71** *

Bran watches the strange creatures race toward him. A net about ten feet wide is spread between them and it is about seven feet off the ground. Bran braces himself. He must cut the net at just the right angle or he will be trapped like a fly in a web.

His sword flashes in the light, and at first Bran thinks he's succeeded. The blade slides through three feet, but then tangles in the net. It's not enough. He is jerked off his feet and the net binds him. Vainly he tries to struggle free, but the net is lined with tiny hooks that catch both armor and flesh. The pain from the hooks is strangely numbing. As the creatures drag Bran across the rocks, he cannot really feel the damage he knows they are causing. Suddenly he realizes there must be poison on the hooks and he cannot defeat it.

Section 72

The drug takes full effect and Bran loses consciousness.

Roll 1 D6 to determine the amount of damage that Bran takes.

Then turn to section 76.

* **72** *

Bran tries to roll off the plate, but he is too late. The floor is vibrating strangely. He feels the vibration reach through the ground, through his feet, till his whole body is shaking. There is pain, but less immediate pain than a throbbing through his body that when completed will leave him in agony. Before he can even identify the pain the young warrior passes out.

Roll 1 D6 to determine the hit points of damage Bran suffers from the electrified plate.

If this brings his hit points to zero, turn to section 29.

If he still has hit points remaining, turn to section 76.

* **73** *

The two enter the dusty passage carefully, wary of traps. The hall winds about like a snake, no doors or passages lead off of it. They follow it for ten minutes before it joins a wide hallway.

The hallway is lined with burning torches. From the end of the passageway Bran and Neal can see two great gold-leafed doors: the entrance to the wizard's workroom. Surprisingly there are no apparent guards. Cautiously they approach the great doors.

No one challenges them. Bran stands before the golden doors. There is no handle. How will they get inside? His thought is answered as the doors open noiselessly by themselves.

"Welcome, Bran O'Neal," says a voice. "It is time you and I met face to face."

Turn to section 66.

* **74** *

Bran decides to try the road. It seems too likely that the mines will be guarded and the stream seems to have only a small chance of success. Bran expects that the road will be guarded, but it is unlikely that the wizard would expect a frontal attack by two travelers and attempting the unexpected always improves the chance of surprise.

So the two will set off the next day.

Bran has no chance to see Maeve that night and he longs to see her just one more time. He is older now. His adventures have taught him much and he knows that he might never again see the woman who has captured his heart.

Fergus and his wife come to see the two adventurers off. The parting is brief and quick. While he knows that the sooner they are off the better and the fewer people who know they're gone the safer they'll be, still Bran can't quite hide his disappointment that Maeve is not there to say farewell.

Lady Margaret says, "Maeve asked me to give you this." She hands Bran a long scarf. "A fitting token for a noble knight."

Bran bows deeply, breathing in the fragrance Maeve has left on the scarf, then he and Neal take their leave.

"Ah, 'tis good to be on the road again, eh, lad?" Neal says, but Bran has no answer for him. He holds the scarf in his fist, his thoughts far from the adventure ahead.

They stop at midday. The road leading to the wizard's stronghold is only half a mile away. From here the companions will walk beside the road, keeping a good distance from it.

The day goes quickly, though the going is hard. The mountains here have been shaped by some strange wind and the rocks are twisted in bizarre forms. Periodically the two can see figures, riding or marching on the road, but none approach.

"I cannot credit it," Neal says, "we're less than two miles away from the black dog's castle and still no one's in sight."

"Who would wish to be in this desolate land?" Bran answers.

"Capture them!" a third voice cries.

"I should learn to hold my tongue," Neal answers. The two companions whirl and see three strange creatures approaching them. They are like centaurs except that they have the bodies of mountain lions not horses. Two, holding the edges of a large net, race toward Bran. The third, moving toward Neal, carries a smaller net.

They move so fast that Neal has no time to use his bow. Bran knows he will have only one chance. He holds his long sword high in both hands and waits for the attack. If he can sever the net he can fight the creatures. There's no chance of avoiding the net, the creatures move too fast.

Roll 3 D6 twice. Once against Bran's Dexterity and then against his Strength.

If the total of the rolls is less than or equal to both Bran's Dexterity value and his Strength value, turn to section 62.

If the total is greater than either value, turn to section 71.

* **75** *

Bran's short sword stabs at the creature's chest. Its webbed hand strikes the sword away. The creature is incredibly strong and the shock of the blow to his sword hand is so great that Bran loses hold of the weapon. He stumbles back, out of the way of the creature's next swing. One of Neal's black arrows hits the monster in the chest. The shot doesn't seem to do much damage, but it does force the monster to step back and give Bran time to recover.

Bran doesn't try to regain his short sword—there is no time. His long sword strikes like a snake. The sword skids along the creature's scales. It slams a fist into the warrior and Bran feels as if his chest has caved in.

He barely manages to dodge the next few blows. Neal's arrows continue to bounce harmlessly off the monster, and Bran knows he cannot avoid the terrible strength of the monster for much longer. He must do something.

He gets up again, his sword moving like a living thing in his hand. Over and over he delivers what should be mortal blows, but the creature's scales are stronger than any armor made. Desperately Bran tries to think of alternatives. The monster must have some weak point.

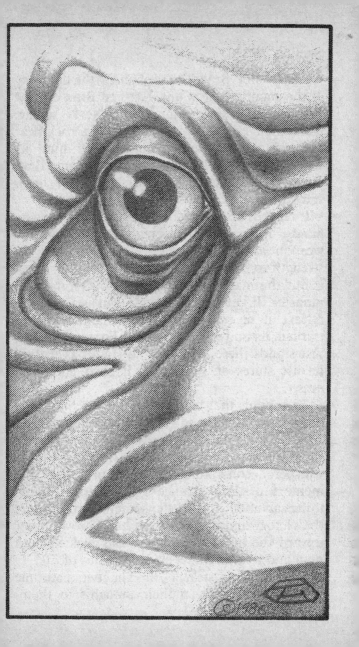

"The water, Bran," Neal shouts, "the lightning of the gauntlet, the water." At first Bran doesn't understand. Then he realizes what Neal is saying. He maneuvers till he is standing on a rock near the water. The creature comes after him, its webbed feet in the water of the stream. Bran activates the gauntlet and slashes at the monster's head.

It reaches up and grabs the sword with both its hands. Bran fears the creature will pull the weapon away from him. It certainly has the strength to.

But the magic of the gauntlet overcomes the monster. It catches the sword, but is unable to release it or pull away as the lightning races through its body into the water. For a moment it just stands there. It makes no sound as it dies. It just stares at Bran with its two great fish eyes.

Bran holds that terrible gaze as the monster's eyes begin to melt, and suddenly it collapses. The water reclaims the creature and Bran recovers his short sword. He does not respond to Neal's whispered congratulations. He can't shake the memory of those strange eyes. There is something sad about this battle, something that sours the victory and makes Bran's heart grow harder toward the black wizard who has twisted both man and animal to his cruel parodies of life.

The castle is near now. The two continue toward it. They keep their thoughts to themselves, but both hold their weapons with white-knuckled intensity.

Turn to section 81.

* **76** *

Bran wakes to a strange swaying motion. At first he is unsure where he is and keeps his eyes closed so as not to reveal that he is awake. He hears the sounds of people around him. His hands and feet are bound to something, a wooden shaft, probably a thick spear.

Slowly he opens one eye. His first sight is of one of the wizard's twisted guardsmen balancing one end of the shaft over his shoulder; another guardsman holds the other end. Bran can see two other guardsmen carrying Neal in a similar fashion. He has no idea where they are going but it seems likely to be toward a quick and evil death. He must escape!

His armor and weapons have been taken from him, but not the gauntlet. With his left hand he activates the magic gift. There is a biting pain in his hand, like that of the councillor's knife, but Bran stoically bears it. In moments the rope binding him to the shaft begins to smoke. None of the guards seem to notice.

Bran waits a few more precious seconds. At

any moment the creatures could become aware of his plan and defeat it all with a quick knife thrust. The rope is nearly burned through. Bran breaks the bindings with a heave. He tucks his head as his back slams into the ground. The guardsmen carrying him lose their balance because of the sudden shift of weight.

Bran places his hands on the ground, lifts himself up into a handstand, and gives a quick twist of his body, spinning both his legs and the attached spear. The spear trips the two creatures. Bran rolls back down and withdraws the spear from between his feet. Quickly he spins the weapon around, loosening the rope around his ankles. He regains his feet and stabs the first guard.

It has been less than thirty seconds and Bran feels a rush of vitality. He is an O'Neal. He shall not die a captive, but as a warrior on his feet, and if this is his day to die, he will bring many along with him to Hell.

Bran has lost his armor. From now on in battle add +1 to anyone's chance to hit him. He does only half the damage he usually does the first two battle rounds of this fight. Bran's hit points are the same as when he was captured.

SOLDIERS
To hit Bran: 14   To be hit: 11   Hit points: 5
Damage with sword: 1 D6−1   Damage with spear: 2 D6

There are four soldiers.

If Bran wins the fight, turn to section 80.

If he loses, turn to section 70.

* 77 *

The floor opens up to swallow the two adventurers, but Bran's quick thinking saves them. Their leaps carry them over the now open pit. Regaining his feet, Bran looks behind them. The pit is ten feet across and twenty straight down. He smells something strange.

"We've got to hurry, boy," Neal whispers. "That trap probably set off some alarm." Bran turns back to the cavern ahead. No reason to worry about stealth now.

The two burst into the cavern. It is a natural cave thirty by sixty feet. The red light is given off by the skull lanterns which hang from the walls at about ten-foot intervals. There is no one here. Three openings lead out.

"Which way?" Bran asks. Neal runs to each, listening carefully. Quickly he points to the one on the right. Bran follows.

"Guards coming up the middle way," Neal says, running alongside Bran, "and something really nasty was to the left. Smelled almost as bad as a human."

Bran does not bother to reply. He recognizes this passage from Fergus's map. It is one of the lesser passages through the mines. Many passages lead off of it. The whole place is a complicated maze, but Bran and Neal studied the maps carefully and can move quickly through the many twists and turns of their path.

Twice they confront the wizard's inhuman guards, and each time Bran and Neal cut the creatures down before they can react. The paths they follow now are rarely used, and they keep up their hectic pace for the next hour.

Finally they stop to catch their breath. They are in a long-abandoned, unlit passage, but Neal carries one of the horrible skull lanterns and it casts light enough for the two.

"Not far now, boy," Neal says. "This passageway will lead us nearly to the castle."

Bran nods, pleased that Fergus's information has been so good. "We'll have to dig our way out," Bran replies. "Fergus said that the opening was closed years ago."

"We'll manage," Neal says. "With my brain and your muscle 'tis as good as done." Neal leads the way, holding the lantern in front of him. After twenty minutes the two come to a dead end. The passage here is full of rocks and debris. Neal waves toward the end of the blocked passage.

"Well, boy, time to dig." He sits down and folds his arms, smiling up at Bran.

Sullenly Bran moves to the passage and begins

to dig, wondering why he brought the elf along in the first place. Surprisingly it takes only a few minutes for Bran to dig through the soft earth and make an opening wide enough for the two to slip through. They find themselves in a spot about a quarter mile above the plain of the wizard's stronghold.

The valley beneath them looks surprisingly pleasant, much like the secret valley Fergus uses as his stronghold. The area is filled with trees and thick shrubs. A great wall at least a mile long loops about the valley, ending at the mountainside. Bran smiles. At least they don't have to run and scale the wall, which he can see is heavily patrolled by the wizard's guards.

The wizard's keep is perched upon a small hill. Its walls are high and many towered. There is constant traffic between it and the small town huddled beneath the great walls. This town is laid out like a chess board and seems to be mostly barracks for the wizard's troops. Bran looks up at the sky.

"It'll be dark soon," he whispers to Neal. "We'll move on to the keep then."

Neal just nods and the two huddle beneath an outcropping of rock, trying to rest a bit. They know that the end of their adventure, for good or ill, is near at hand.

Turn to section 81.

* **78** *

Bran hears a strange whining sound from the walls, and the floor beneath him begins to vibrate. He tucks and rolls off of the metal plate and onto the regular stone floor. Neal leaps over the trap to land at the warrior's side.

"That was close," Bran whispers.

"When, by all that's holy," Neal answers, "when are you going to learn to watch where you're going?" Bran ignores the elf, not bothering to mention that Neal didn't see the trap either.

The adventurers move to the end of the corridor. They stare at two branching corridors. The one to the left is dusty, narrow, and full of cobwebs. The other is clean; bright torches hang from engraved sconces along its length. The two hesitate. One of these hallways leads to the wizard's workroom, the other—who knows?

If Bran takes the dusty corridor, turn to section 73.

If he takes the clean corridor, turn to section 79.

* **79** *

The passage the two enter is absolutely straight. Its dimensions are perfect. The walls and floor are made of great slabs of black rock. Bran looks around nervously, searching for signs of a trap.

Neal tugs on Bran's leg and points to the walls. Bran can see a groove two inches wide cut into the wall which goes from the ceiling to a point one foot from the ground. There are several other identical grooves both along that wall and parallel on the other wall. There are grooves every two feet, and they continue for four feet down the hall in both directions.

It means something, Bran is sure.

Roll 3 D6.

If the roll is less than or equal to Bran's Wisdom/ Luck value, turn to Section 86.

If it is greater than Bran's Wisdom/Luck value, turn to section 98.

✻ **80** ✻

Bran catches the first guard unawares and the spear goes straight through the creature's neck, killing it instantly. Bran spins to face the creature that carried the front of the spear. It raises a sword and, howling, attacks. Bran deflects the sword blow with the end of the spear. He cuts through the creature's thigh, a deep, disabling wound. Then he spins again to face the other two guardsmen who have dropped Neal to face Bran. A third guardsman has joined them.

Bran throws the spear, catching the lead creature full in the chest. The other two hesitate. Bran spins down and picks up the sword dropped by the guard he wounded. He realizes with a thrill that it is his own long sword and with it in hand, he leaps at the howling guards.

The battle is over in seconds. Never has the young warrior fought with such surety and savagery. Bran slits the throats of the wounded. The battle began and ended so quickly that no alarm has been raised. Bran makes his way to Neal and cuts him free.

"Neal . . . Neal," he whispers, "are you well?" For a moment there is no answer. Then the elf opens his eyes, giving Bran an exaggerated wink.

"Some hero you are," he says. "Took you long enough to escape."

"Get up, you laggard." Bran's pretended exasperation cannot hide his pleasure at seeing the elf unhurt. "We have a wizard to see."

The two quickly realize they are within the wizard's castle. They had feared that during their captivity they had been taken farther from their goal. Instead, they realize, they are scant yards away. At last, Bran thinks, the end of the quest, and the answers to all the riddles.

The two re-arm themselves and move down the dark corridor. They know from Fergus's map that this passage will lead them to the wizard's workroom. It is a dusty and deserted-looking corridor, dark and damp. Quickly they enter it. The end is in sight.

If up to this point Bran still retained his chainmail, it is now gone. He refits himself with armor from the dead guards but this fits so poorly it gives him no bonuses. Also lost are any potions he carried with him. He does, however, recover both his long sword and his brother's short sword, and he still has the gauntlet.

Turn to section 73.

* **81** *

Bran and Neal approach the wizard's castle stealthily, staying well away from the road that leads to the main gate. There is no secret passage into the place; this time they must go over the wall. They make their way to the east wall.

In the shadow of the wall Bran withdraws a rope and grapple. The metal grapple is covered with thick felt to muffle its sound when it strikes the wall. Murmuring a quiet prayer he swings the grapple three times around and then with a grunt lets it fly to the top of the wall. There is a dull clunk. He draws on the rope, pulling it tight and testing to make certain that the grapple is set securely enough to bear his weight.

Bran holds the rope still as Neal quickly scampers up it. To Bran it seems as if Neal fairly flies up the wall, hardly touching the rope at all. For a moment there is silence, then Bran feels a jerk on the rope. Carefully he scales the wall.

Neal waits for him at the top. Beside him lies the body of one of the wizard's guards, his throat cut. Neal just shrugs at Bran's look. Bran pulls up the rope. From here they can follow Fergus's directions and hopefully catch the wizard alone in his workroom.

Neal secures the rope on the battlements with a complicated knot. The two use it to aid their climb down the parapets, then Neal tugs twice on the line. The rope unties itself and falls at his feet.

"Pretty neat trick, eh?" the elf whispers. Bran just smiles, leading the way toward the main house in the keep. The dark provides them with plenty of hiding places and the few sentries are easily avoided. They come to a thick iron-studded door. According to Fergus's map this leads into the main kitchen. Bran just stares at it in silence. How is he supposed to get through?

By punching the warrior's knee, Neal pushes Bran aside, then moves to the door and murmurs to himself for a moment. There is a sharp click, and the door opens. Neal gestures for Bran to go ahead of him again.

"You're full of tricks," Bran mumbles.

"I'm full of more than tricks, me boyo," the elf answers. Bran refrains from giving the obvious reply.

As they were told, behind the door is a short passage that leads into the main kitchen. Bran and Neal move quietly through this area to avoid waking the serfs sleeping in the corners of the room. Like two shadows the warriors drift through the silent corridors of the castle, none aware of their presence.

After a half hour the companions reach a main hall. In the fitful light of the torches that dot the castle halls, they can see that the passage branches to the right and left a hundred yards farther on.

"I don't remember this from the map," Bran whispers. Neal nods in agreement. Bran steps out to lead the way. But the floor has changed somehow. Looking down he realizes he has stepped on a metal plate inset in the floor. Again he has blundered into a trap.

Roll 3 D6.

If the total is less than or equal to Bran's Intelligence value, turn to section 78.

If the total is greater than his Intelligence, turn to section 72.

* **82** *

Bran wastes no time trying to determine how Balar set the arrow on fire. Charging at the wizard, the young warrior cries his clan's war cry. "O'Neal!"

For a moment Balar seems to hesitate. And in a flash of inspiration Bran knows why: The wizard has some reason to fear the O'Neals. But the mage quickly recovers. He points his finger at Bran, crying out some arcane word. Bran feels a force slam into his chest, lifting him off his feet. Instead of resisting the magic Bran uses its force to push off into a back flip, and with a twist he lands back on his feet like a cat. Again he charges.

Balar pulls a black ball out of a hidden pocket. The ball levitates above the mage's head and Balar cries another arcane word. This time the effect is quite different. The ball bursts into flame and shoots straight at Bran. The warrior is unable to dodge the fireball completely and he is forced to roll in order to put out his cloak which caught fire.

But in concentrating on Bran, Balar has forgotten Neal and the elf fires three of his arrows in quick succession. Again the wizard's magic renders the bolts useless, but in the intervening time Bran regains his feet and this time he manages to move within sword range.

Bran's long sword comes down in a sweeping arc aimed at the wizard's neck. But in midstroke some force intervenes and stops the sword's movement. At the same time the wizard casts another spell. This time a dazzling kaleidoscope of lights bursts in the air between the two antagonists, and the flare momentarily blinds Bran. The wizard begins to laugh.

The wizard's laugh is cut short when Bran's short sword slices through his chest. Long is the training the heirs of the O'Neals must go through in order to gain their fighting skills, and many are the times that such practices are held blindfolded or in the dark.

Still, the wizard doesn't die, and again Bran is struck a stunning blow by an unseen force. This time it hits his head and the warrior falls to his knees. But Bran does not lose his grip on his short sword. He pushes the weapon deeper into the wizard's body. At the same time he drops his long sword and uses his free hand to catch the mage behind a knee and flip him onto his back.

The wizard, in desperation, creates another fireball. Bran tries to break his enemy's concentration with an elbow in the stomach, but he misses his target. The fireball crashes full onto the warrior's back.

Bran rolls off the wizard and onto his back to put out the flames. As he does Neal leaps in to attack the wizard, but Balar has already regained his feet. An unseen force hits the elf in midleap and smashes him into a wall twenty feet away. Neal goes limp.

Bran tries to regain his feet, but his head is still pounding. He can't concentrate. Another fireball hits him, this time full in the chest. Pain bursts through the battle fog and Bran cries out involuntarily. Again, the unseen force crashes into him. The wizard's laughter is the only thing the warrior can hear, its sound vibrating through Bran's wounds, striking them like a razor.

Turn to section 29.

* **83** *

Bran lunges at Donal, his weapons spinning. Donal meets him with the same form. The four swords whirl and crash. Every attack Bran attempts is parried by the uncommonly strong wizard. But Bran's rage sustains him as the two duel across the room.

Bran hears weapons pounding on the barred door which Neal is guarding. Bran knows it is only a matter of time till the wizard's reinforcements break through. Then he and Neal will be dead men for sure.

Bran uses what little witchcraft he can manage, but that, too, is easily repelled by the wizard. Donal replies with a magical blow to try to knock Bran's guard aside. But the warrior will not be thwarted so easily.

Bran feels tired. Both he and Donal are covered with blood from the blades' flashing bites. Donal's defense is slowly shattering. He has learned the fighting skill, but in the history of the O'Neals there has been no finer warrior than Bran, and his superior skill is beginning to tell. But he is so tired that he cannot afford a long battle. He must kill the wizard quickly. He must kill him now.

Bran lunges. His sword goes through the wizard's chest but misses the heart, a slight miscal-

Section 84

culation, but the last one the warrior will ever make. The Reaper crashes down on his head, cutting through scalp, bone, and brain. Bran falls, his father's sword imbedded in his skull. Even in death the irony is not lost on Bran. The sword is well named.

Turn to section 29.

* **84** *

The floor opens beneath the two companions. Bran leaps but not far enough. He slams into the side of the now-revealed pit and, unable to stop himself, slides to the bottom. It is a long drop and he hits hard. Neal lands on top of him.

Beneath their feet is a thick and dry substance. It fills the area with unpleasant fumes though it gives off no heat. Bran feels light-headed all of a sudden. He knows something is wrong; the fall wasn't sufficient to effect him so greatly. He grabs for the side of the pit, but his balance is all wrong and he crashes to the floor. It must be the strange stuff coating the bottom of the pit that is making him so dizzy. He must get away. But his understanding is too late, and he loses all concerns as he loses consciousness.

Roll 1 D6. Bran takes half the damage rolled.

Turn to section 76.

* **85** *

Before the rat-thing can bound closer, one of Neal's black arrows hits it full in the chest. The monster stares at the shaft dumbly for a moment. Bran takes advantage of the creature's momentary confusion and attacks.

His swords blur again, the long one glowing with the magic of the gauntlet. He dares two slashes, one across the chest, one across a furred arm, and then leaps out of the creature's reach. Again and again Bran dodges in to make two quick cuts. But the rat creature seems immune to pain, and says nothing more during the fight.

It lumbers across the room, trying to force Bran into a corner, but the young warrior is too nimble. Though the creature's claws do score more than once, the damage they cause is not serious. The monster seems totally immune to Neal's arrows which soon are covering it thickly and Bran's own blows seem to do little more good.

"How do we kill this thing?" Bran shouts. But Neal answers with a shrug. Bran is beginning to tire. He must end the fight soon. With that thought he rolls behind the creature. He is on his feet before the rat-thing can respond and Bran's two blades descend on its neck in a cross-cut. The creature's head falls to the ground. For a

moment more the body continues to stumble around, then it, too, falls.

"It'll be a cold day in Hell when Neal O'Neal is eaten by an overgrown rat," Neal says, methodically retrieving his arrows from the monster's corpse. Bran picks up the torch and begins to look around. The room is large, about twenty feet by thirty. At the far end there is a doorway. In one of the corners is a lump of garbage which the rat obviously used as its nest. Not all the bones there belonged to animals.

"Well, looks like we go that way," Bran says.

Neal heads toward the doorway with a shrug. "Lucky," he says, "this place wasn't guarded."

Bran doesn't bother to answer. The doorway leads to a narrow passage carved through the rock of the mountain. Silently the two move onward.

Turn to section 67.

* **86** *

Bran looks above him. The ceiling here is one black stone slab that goes from the start of the groove to the end.

"Run!" he yells and races down the hall. He hears a grinding noise above him, but he doesn't take the time to look. He skids to a halt ten feet away. Behind him the ceiling stone has slid down the grooves, stopping a foot above the floor. An ingenious trap that would not crush, but would injure and trap anyone caught beneath it. He looks down at Neal.

"Too close," he says. Neal points to the end of the hall where it joins another large hallway. Bran can see two golden doors not ten feet down the passageway.

"Very close," Neal whispers. "The door to the dark one's lair." The two look at each other. Then with no further speech they move to the gold-leafed doors.

Strangely, they are not guarded. Indeed, there is no one to be seen anywhere in the large hallway. It is as if the whole castle were empty.

"How do we get in?" Bran murmurs, for there are no handles on the great doors. As if in answer to his question the doors silently open on their own.

"Welcome, Bran O'Neal," a voice says. "It is time that you and I met face to face."

Turn to section 66.

Turn to section 66.

* **87** *

Though Bran wants to help Fergus free his wife, the young warrior feels that he must lead the attack on the wall. The fighting at the wall will be especially dangerous and his chivalry demands that he fight where he will be most needed. Besides, if the clan war cry is going to be used there, then an O'Neal should be one of the leaders.

Both Neal and Fergus approve of his choice and Bran moves to the north side where the attack will take place. Here are three hundred of Fergus's men led by two captains and augmented by five of the elite guard. One hundred ladders lay stacked neatly, ready for the attack to come.

Quickly Bran takes command and issues the ladders to the men. The five elite guard immediately attach themselves to the young warrior. Bran tries not to stare at the warriors; they are a strange group. Some seem to be part monkey or dog, while one has the body of a snake, with two arms and a complete human head. All are eager for revenge for the evil that was done to them.

Bran watches the sky carefully. Still he almost misses the moment, but Neal kicks him and Bran leaps to his feet, drawing his blades.

"O'Neal!" he cries.

"O'Neal!" the army shouts at his back, and the cry echoes through the mountains. Bran races ahead, leading the men to the wall as arrows begin to fill the skies. But Bran ignores them, his head still spinning with the ancient war cry of the clan. If only Sean could see him. Sean, he thinks, I am coming. I will avenge you, my brother.

Section 87

The warriors reach the wall and the ladders smack onto it with a loud crack. Quickly the men begin scrambling up, their weapons waving in the light of the dawn. Bran clambers up one, the elite guard scrambling up behind him. One of the castle soldiers reaches out to push the ladder aside, but Bran throws his short sword, catching the creature in the throat. He is over the wall in seconds, drawing his brother's short sword. Once more his double blades flash, and the enemy falls about him.

The fighting is fierce. In the initial moments of the attack Bran's men catch the enemy almost completely off guard and several groups manage to clear the wall about them. But now the wizard's strange soldiers are rallying and warriors are engaged in single combat all across the ten-foot-wide parapet. Neal appears on the battlements next to Bran, his tiny bow taking a lethal toll of the enemy. Then, once more, Bran hears the cry of O'Neal as the main gates crash down and Fergus leads his warriors into the main court of the castle.

Bran can see the giant, his ax sweeping all opponents out of the way.

"Shall we join him?" Neal cries behind him. Bran must decide quickly. The men on the walls are well organized and follow their own captain. They don't seem to need him to lead them. He could join Fergus, who even now is moving toward the main hall. But where is he needed most, here on the walls, or with Fergus?

Roll 3 D6 against Bran's Constitution. If the total is greater than Bran's Constitution value, then take 1 D6 hit points from his total for the wounds he suffered while attacking the wall. If the total is less than or equal to Bran's Constitution value, then Bran has managed not to take any wounds. If this brings Bran's total to 0, turn to section 29.

If Bran joins Fergus, turn to section 64.

If Bran stays with the soldiers on the wall, turn to section 47.

* **88** *

The path slowly begins to get rockier. Suddenly a shadow covers Bran and he looks up to a horrid sight.

There, standing before him, is a creature at least eight feet tall. It is vaguely human but massively deformed: one arm withered and useless, the other thick and obscenely muscled. Clutched in that terrible arm is a thick stone club with jagged edges. The creature's skin is tough and covered with patches of different color hide. It wears an old wolf pelt as a loin cloth. Its thick, tree-stump legs are hairy like an animal's. But it is its face that is truly horrifying.

Its head is oblong and forms into a small snout where two great canines surrounded by pointed brown teeth glare at him in a parody of a smile. The face is patched and quilted in reds and browns as if someone had sewn skin on it from fifty different animals. And its eyes are yellow.

"Manfood," it hisses, "manfood," and it raises its club above its head. Bran draws his swords. A troll, he thinks, good God, a troll, and with that he prepares to fight for his life.

TROLL
*To hit Bran: 10   To be hit: 14   Hit points: 18
Damage with club: 1 D6   Damage with swords: 1
D6+2*

If Bran wins the fight with the troll, turn to section 7.

If Bran loses the fight with the troll, turn to section 90.

* **89** *

The monster moves closer, and Bran waits to learn its method of attack. The creature is now within ten feet of the warrior. Its gait, out of the water, is awkward and slow. But the head—Bran knows that is the danger.

The creature hisses at him, revealing the rows of jagged teeth in its small snout. Then the head dips down with the speed of a lightning bolt. Bran avoids the teeth, but is bowled over when the creature whips its head back up, smacking Bran in the shoulder. Quickly the dragon attacks again, and again, and again.

Bran loses all conscious thought as he just reacts to his opponent's inhuman speed. His vision is filled with the snapping mouth and the one angry, soulless eye. Again and again Bran's swords cut deep into the creature's leather hide, but to little purpose. His blows seem only to enrage the dragon.

Bran is tiring fast, the footing is treacherous, but he must at all costs avoid the dragon's teeth. He sees a good example of how powerful those jaws are, when the dragon, missing Bran, snaps a chunk out of a tree in its rage. But Bran does see a chance. The creature, for all its speed, has poor aim, probably due to the fact that it has only one eye. More importantly, the neck, while incredibly flexible, has a limited range of movement. The creature can strike anything in front of it or to the side, but it seems unable to turn to protect itself against attacks from the rear.

Gambling everything on one move Bran dodges, and as the creature's head rears back up into striking position, Bran leaps up in an attempt to jump right over the back of the creature. But just as Bran's feet are about to clear the dragon's back, its neck turns to the side and knocks Bran to the ground with its head. Before Bran can regain his feet, he sees the creature open wide its huge jaws, its jagged teeth gleaming, and start to snap them down on Bran.

Turn to section 29.

* **90** *

The troll's first blow misses Bran, smashing into the earth where he stood moments before. The skull is smashed into a thousand splinters. Before the monster can recover, Bran slashes it across its left leg with his long sword. Thick red blood slowly leaks from the wound, but the creature does not seem to notice.

Again and again its great club slashes at Bran, time and again he ducks under the blow or nimbly avoids it. His weapons reach out to cut the monster on its legs, its chest, its back, but still the creature attacks, its bellows of outrage nearly deafening the young warrior.

Bran knows that if the troll manages to hit him, he is a dead man. The power in the creature's arm is unbelievable. Bran is nearly caught when one of the creature's wild blows slams into a young pine, breaking it like a twig and nearly trapping Bran beneath the tree as it falls. Bran ducks in, out, cuts, slashes, dives, rolls. He calls up every trick he has, whether martial or magical, to use against the monster. And still it will not die.

Finally Bran is backed against another tree. He is tired and bruised and the monster has come close to killing him more than once. He watches with dread as the ponderous creature approaches. The troll swings his club directly at Bran's head. Bran blocks the swing with his long sword, but the troll's strength is too much for him and Bran's arm is forced back. Suddenly the troll butts his head into Bran's stomach and he doubles over in pain. As he begins to straighten up he sees the club about to descend on his head.

Turn to section 29.

* **91** *

The monster bends its legs and with one great leap attacks Bran. The warrior ducks under the attack, rolling to one side. But he doesn't escape unscathed. One of the claws on the spider's leg cuts him across the face.

Bran gets back on his feet just as the monster pounces again. This time Bran rushes to meet the monster, and his short sword scores a wound under the creature's belly. But once more Bran fails to avoid one of the claws. The two continue their bizarre dance of death for some time, and both are spattered with blood.

Neal stands some twenty feet away from the two combatants. He takes aim and rapidly fires his thin black arrows. Unfortunately the arrows seem to have little effect. Though he has managed to hit the monster several times, it seems unaffected by its wounds.

In desperation Bran changes his attack. Instead of aiming for the body, he focuses on the monster's legs. As the creature leaps again, Bran dodges to one side. His long sword flashes out in an arc and severs the claw from one leg of the monster. At first it seems unaffected by the wound, but when it next tries to attack, it stumbles on its injured leg.

Bran darts in three more times, each time

severing a claw. The creature begins to lose its balance but manages to thrust a large rock at Bran, catching the warrior off guard. The missile catches him in the shoulder, his left arm goes numb, and his short sword falls from nerveless fingers and clatters to the ground. One of the spider's legs thrusts out and its claw rips across Bran's throat, severing his windpipe. The pain is intense as Bran starts to lose consciousness.

Turn to section 29.

* **92** *

Bran knows he must take the fight to the soldiers or he is a dead man for sure. He waits till the hill has slowed their charge a bit, then rushes to meet the warriors halfway.

Tucking into a roll to dodge a sword, Bran comes out of it to slice his long sword across a horse's back legs. The animal falls and several of the warriors can't swerve in time. They are caught in the tangle as the crippled animal thrashes about in agony, crushing its rider beneath its weight.

Bran leaps over the mess and straight into another soldier, knocking the man off his horse. As the two fall together, Bran shifts so his enemy lands beneath him. Even as the wind is knocked out of the soldier, Bran slits the man's throat.

Section 92

Bran scrambles back to his feet, whirling his sword to block a cut coming straight for him. Before Bran can attack, the soldier drops from his saddle, a small arrow jutting from his neck. Neal is doing his part.

The battlefield is in confusion now, with the downed horse still struggling to get up. The three remaining soldiers try to ride Bran down, but the warrior is too quick for them. Another falls to an elven arrow, and Bran takes down one with a slash that cuts through mail, leather, and stomach.

Now only the leader remains.

"Die!" he shouts, and rides straight for Bran. The man catches another of Neal's arrows on his shield and continues to bear down on Bran. Bran barely deflects the leader's sword stroke, and the horse, well trained, gives him a glancing blow with its front hooves as its rider turns to attack again. Three times the two warriors clash, three times Bran barely beats him back. Each time Bran finds it harder and harder to raise his arms to fight. As the soldier comes in again, Bran attempts to block the soldier's sword with his short sword, but he is too weary. The soldier's sword slashes down on Bran's wrist and he drops his sword. The soldier darts his sword in and pierces Bran through the heart.

Turn to section 29.

* 93 *

Brans lunges at the closing entrance, but he has failed to hold his breath and the poison gas has already taken its toll on him. His reflexes and perception are off and Bran only succeeds in hitting his head on the closing panel. The door slams shut with a clang and Bran is trapped in a room full of poison green gas.

Turn to section 29.

* 94 *

Realizing that the green gas is probably poison, Bran holds his breath, but unfortunately his lunge at the closing entrance is a moment too late. The door slams shut with a clang and Bran is trapped in a room full of poison green gas.

Turn to section 29.

* **95** *

Bran and Neal wait for the giant gremlins to attack. Neal brings down one with an arrow in its eye, and then the true battle begins. In the confusion of the melee Bran loses sight of Neal as he fights for his life.

The monsters are armed with clubs mostly. Two have spears, but they seem inexperienced in their use. Bran's swords flash, and the second of the gremlins falls, its stomach opened by the dancing weapons. The remaining eight split up and two charge Neal while the other six advance on Bran. While Bran concentrates on using his swords on the three to the right, left, and center; the three others start pummeling him from the back with their clubs. Bran whirls to meet their attack, but is again assaulted by the others. It does not take long for the odds to overwhelm Bran and he begins to lose consciousness.

Turn to section 29.

* **96** *

Before the rat-thing can bound closer, one of Neal's black arrows hits it full in the chest. The monster stares at the shaft dumbly for a moment. Bran takes advantage of the creature's momentary confusion and attacks.

His swords blur again, the long one glowing with the magic of the gauntlet. He dares two slashes, one across the chest, one across a furred arm, and then leaps out of the creature's reach. Again and again Bran dodges in to make two quick cuts. But the rat creature seems immune to pain, and says nothing more during the fight.

It lumbers across the room, trying to force Bran into a corner, but the young warrior is too nimble. Though the creature's claws do score more than once, the damage they cause is not serious. The monster seems totally immune to Neal's arrows which soon are covering it thickly and Bran's own blows seem to do little more good.

"How do we kill this thing?" Bran shouts. But Neal answers with a shrug. Bran is beginning to tire. He must end the fight soon. Bran tucks into a roll to get behind the creature, but the rat-thing whips out a paw and slashes its claws across Bran's back. The pain is intense. Bran stumbles to his feet, but once again the rat-thing's claws strike out and cut deeply into his chest. Bran sinks to the ground knowing it's the end.

Turn to section 29.

* **97** *

Bran's short sword stabs at the creature's chest. Its webbed hand strikes the sword away. The creature is incredibly strong and the shock of the blow to his sword hand is so great that Bran loses hold of the weapon. He stumbles back, out of the way of the creature's next swing. One of Neal's black arrows hits the monster in the chest. The shot doesn't seem to do much damage, but it does force the monster to step back and give Bran time to recover.

Bran doesn't try to regain his short sword—there is no time. His long sword strikes like a snake. The sword skids along the creature's scales. It slams a fist into the warrior and Bran feels as if his chest has caved in.

He barely manages to dodge the next few blows. Neal's arrows continue to bounce harmlessly off the monster, and Bran knows he cannot avoid the terrible strength of the monster for much longer. He must do something.

He gets up again, his sword moving like a living thing in his hand. Over and over he delivers what should be mortal blows, but the creature's scales are stronger than any armor made. Desperately Bran tries to think of alternatives. The monster must have some weak point.

"The water, Bran," Neal shouts, "the lightning of the gauntlet, the water." At first Bran doesn't understand. Then he realizes what Neal is saying. He maneuvers till he is standing on a rock near the water. The creature comes after him, its webbed feet in the water of the stream. Bran activates the gauntlet and slashes at the monster's head.

It reaches up and grabs the sword with both its hands. Before the lightning from the gauntlet has a chance to effect the monster, it pulls the sword from out of Bran's hands. Caught off balance on the slippery rock, Bran tumbles into the water. Before he can surface he feels the monster's fish body on top of him pushing him deeper into the water.

Turn to section 29.

* **98** *

Bran looks above him. The ceiling here is one black stone slab that goes from the start of the groove to the end. He resumes walking when he hears a grinding noise above. He glances up and

Section 98

sees the ceiling stone is sliding down the grooves toward him. He yells, "Run," but he is too late. Before he has a chance to go more than a few feet down the hall, the ceiling stone crashes down on his head, knocking him to the floor.

Turn to section 29.

AUTHORS' BIOGRAPHIES

MARK PERRY IS twenty-five and lives in Michigan. His book, *The Morigu*, has been published by Warner/Questar. He is currently finishing up a horror novel titled *The Fall*. After that he will begin working on the next of the *Morigu* series. He has also been published in various other forms, including a story in *The Blood of Ten Chiefs*.

Mark has had every incredibly stupid and annoying job known to man—most of which he was fired from or quit in the first week. He was surprised to find his B.A. means absolutely nothing in the real world. And graduate school was a poor joke at best. He thinks it is incredibly cool that people pay him to do what he loves and does best: write.

Megahn Perry was born in Richmond, Virginia, nine years ago.

She is a fourth-grade student at John B. Dey Elementary School in Virginia Beach, Virginia.

Her hobbies are writing, drawing, reading, and gymnastics. She loves to travel and gets many opportunities to do so as her family is scattered from Massachusetts to California.

Megahn comes from a very artistic family and hopes to do something in that field when she is older.

She is the mother of eight Cabbage Patch kids.